THE MARBLE ARMY

a novel

GISELE FIRMINO

Outpost19 | San Francisco
outpost19.com

Firmino, Gisele
         Marble Army, The / Gisele Firmino
         ISBN 9781937402792 (pbk)
         ISBN 9781937402808 (ebk)

Library of Congress Control Number: 2015912529

OUTPOST19

ORIGINAL
PROVOCATIVE
READING

THE MARBLE ARMY

For Lorenzo

"as if suddenly the roots I had left behind
cried out to me, the land I had lost with my childhood –
and I stopped, wounded by the wandering scent."
Pablo Neruda

ONE

OUR ONLY HOME was in Minas do Leão.

The house was a salmon colored, two-story cube, with windows on all four sides, which made us feel as though we knew all there was to know about our town and its people. My mother's favorite was the kitchen window, framing the meadow, the mine and beyond.

The first floor was never furnished except for about ten mismatched chairs, a side table and an old mattress, which sat in what was supposed to be our living room. All chairs were arranged in a kind of a semicircle by the fireplace. Pablo and I were the only ones who used the mattress to sit on while playing games, or just hanging out. But we lived on the second floor.

Like every other house in town, its foundation consisted of wood planks holding it above the ground by about a foot or so, the wood flooring was nailed to these planks, not always leveled. Although this system gave a little bounce to our walk, it provided no insulation whatsoever, and very often we'd pluck the weeds that made their way through the seams; half-black, half-bright green intruders. This closeness to the freezing black dirt sent chills through our spines pushing us up to the second floor. But we were *gaúchos*; physically enduring the cold winter was just as expected as the daily rice and beans.

But when summer came, our mother would open up the first floor, arrange flowers throughout, and we'd have picnics on the living room floor as we tried to dodge the heat from upstairs. Chopped watermelon and colonial cheese for Pablo and me, chilled quail eggs and pickles for our parents. With all its strangeness, it was the perfect house to grow up in.

One afternoon I was sitting as close as one could possibly sit to the fireplace without getting burnt, when I heard something thumping downstairs. The sounds were loud against the hollow hardwood floor and seemed to move around as if a giant had invaded our slanted home.

"What's going on?" my mother asked from the kitchen sink.

"Luca!" I heard Pablo's voice coming from the first floor.

Pablo had been in the tool shed the whole day. I had tried to keep him company for a while, but the cold was unbearable. At one point he must have come in without us noticing him. He called me again, screeching even more. At fifteen, his voice was changing. But always self-conscious, Pablo would manage to control it as much as humanly possible.

"Luca! *Vem cá*! *Rápido*!" he kept calling, his words mingled with the thump sounds.

"What are you doing down there, Pablo?" my mother said as she patted her hands against her apron. But before she could say anything else I ran downstairs.

Pablo stood almost a whole meter taller, laughing, and strutting around on top of wooden stilts he had just made. With his long skinny arms draped over them, his feet as high as my waist, he looked like the king of somewhere.

Although he struggled for balance, it seemed as though he'd done this before. I had never seen stilts, and was baffled by his ability to walk around with them. The sun bled through the window curtains, and specks of dust glittered as they swayed within a beam of light, aiming at Pablo's knees. He smiled with pride; his thin body looking even leaner at that height.

"If you're cold, you need to move around. Sitting by the fireplace won't help you one bit!" He managed to look at me for a moment, a twinkle in his hazel eyes. But he was quickly forced to focus on what he was doing.

The stilts were regular two by fours sanded smoothly, thinning at the bottom, and curved on top where Pablo glued foam to protect our armpits. They were perfect!

I heard my mother's steps approaching, and before she could see us and say *no*, I asked Pablo if I could try them. My limbs were shaking from the cold and the rush of anxiety as I realized what I was about to do.

Pablo jumped down from the stilts, and held them straight up for me. His smile was reassuring.

"Here, put one foot here first, put your hand right here," he said as he placed my hand as high as I could reach. "Now pull yourself up. There," he said.

I was taller than him.

"Now put the other foot here," he said, pointing at the other stilt. I did.

"Pablo! I don't think that's a good idea." Our mother stood on the bottom step watching us apprehensively. Her hands tugged her apron against the cold.

"I got you, Luca." He looked me right in the eye. "Don't you worry. I got you."

I glanced at our mother, and she smiled with confidence. She knew Pablo had things under control, and I wondered if I would someday feel what it was like for people to trust you the way she trusted him.

"Focus, Luc," he said. "I'm going to let go now. But I'm close. Don't worry. I've got you."

I didn't worry. But I stayed in place, terrified by the thought of taking my first step. I knew Pablo would catch me if something were to happen, but I just wanted to get it right.

"You have to walk, or else you'll fall," said Pablo, clutching the stilts with his chapped hands.

"I will. I will." I tried taking one step but the stilt got stuck on one of the creases on the floor, and my foot came off of it. But before I could consider the idea of falling, Pablo was there to hold the stilts straight up.

"Oh, I don't know, Pablo," our mother said.

"Luca, look at me." Pablo didn't so much as glance at her. "You have to shift your weight from side to side. These legs aren't yours. You have to make them yours. Lift them with your hands, and make them walk for you."

He let go of one stilt.

"It's fine. You can do it. I know you can," he added.

And just like that I was on my own. I walked around with Pablo behind me. Our mother watched us as we giggled and couldn't contain her smile. The hollow wood floor responded to every step I took, giving in a little, shouting back at me each time I touched base. Pablo gradually distanced himself as I gained confidence and looked at my face instead of my feet. His smile was as big as mine must have been.

. . .

Only three weeks before the dictatorship came to us, there was a big party inaugurating the street that led to the mine. It was a dirt path, really, created within the meadow from all the workers coming and going to their daily shifts. The party would officially turn that path into a street, one that would be named after my father.

Our mother had busied around the house all afternoon with about ten rollers in her hair, leaving behind a trail of powder makeup smell and rose perfume. Her steps were louder than usual against the hollow wood flooring, giving away her excitement.

"Tuck your shirt in, Pablo, and please, please comb your hair, honey," she announced as she walked past us toward the small front balcony facing the main street. Mãe was always humming something, singing parts of songs we didn't really know except from listening to her. I used to think they reflected her mood, as if they could say the things she chose to keep to herself. On that day though she sang the same song, over and over.

"Se essa rua, se essa rua fosse minha
Eu mandava, eu mandava ladrilhar
Com pedrinhas, com pedrinhas de brilhante
Para o meu, para o meu amor passar."

Outside, women carried big casseroles covered with hand-painted dishcloths, while men swept sidewalks, fixed tables with

4

bricks and wood planks, and children buzzed around them like flies, seeking attention.

"Yes! Big day for us!" our mother yelled from the balcony as she pretended to check on the flowerpots instead of the commotion.

"We're so honored!" she said, clasping her hands together, like a character in a Victorian novel.

She took one last look at the street and headed back in. Pablo and I were both sitting by the radio, eating chocolate cigarettes our mother had given us. They came in a pack just like regular cigarettes, wrapped individually. We pretended to listen to the news as we copied the way our father squinted when he took a drag, and how he crossed one leg over the other and leaned back before exhaling, his bare belly more and more noticeable when he relaxed. Then we'd eat it and move on to the next cigarette.

On her way back to her room, our mother stopped to watch us. She took out one of my chocolates and tucked it over her ear, pushing one of her rollers back.

"Long day today," she said with a rasp as she took a seat. "You boys keep quiet, will you?" She forced each word onto the next, the way our father did. Mãe reached for the radio to turn the volume up. "Aaahh…There's so much coal in this place, there's work for your grandchildren here."

She looked straight at us, her shoulders hunched, her brows knitted in a frown, but she couldn't keep the deep tone for too long. Our mother took the cigarette out, pinching it between her delicate thumb and forefinger, her nails painted a deep bright orange for the party. She looked at the cigarette in between her fingers for a moment but broke out with laughter before she could get through the gesture.

We were being *bobos*. Pablo finished another cigarette, turned the volume down, flicked his hair back, and looked at our mother.

"Mãe, can I please just wear it like this? This is how you're supposed to wear your hair nowadays." Our mother stared at

Pablo for a few seconds, considering his plea. "*Por favor?*"

"Does Rita like it like that?" she asked.

"What? I don't know what you're talking about." Pablo shoved a chocolate into his mouth, his cheeks slightly pink.

"Doesn't Rita mind when you wear it messy like that?" she insisted.

"Mãe," Pablo pleaded.

"Sure, honey. You're handsome no matter what." She glanced at her nails. "Besides, we're visionaries, aren't we? At least that's what people say."

While we were home, counting down the minutes to the big party, our father was working as if this was just another day. Mãe grabbed a glass of water from the kitchen and stepped again onto the balcony to water her lilies, taking another glimpse at the street below.

"Such a beautiful day! I can't believe how it cleared up! It will sure be muddy, though," she said as she headed back to the kitchen. "I just hope your father gives himself enough time to clean up." Her voice echoed through the hallway.

The party was on the corner of the city's main street and what would become our father's street – Rua Antonio Fonte. Everybody but those who had the night shift showed up. Each family helped out with something to eat or drink.

While Pablo and I stuffed ourselves with fried chicken thighs dipped in yucca flour, our mother circled through all the cliques with a *cachaça com butiá* in her hand and a tireless smile. Every time she saw someone sipping their own drinks, she would just barely moisten her lips, licking them immediately because she liked the taste but not the burn. Then she would go on repeating herself over and over about what an honor the whole day was. Tio Joca's wife, Ana, had brought a huge tray of cold cuts and cheeses, and also circled around the party with it. The warm and tangy smell of homemade *linguiças*, *morcilhas*, and sausages left a trail behind her. But Pablo and I followed her for the cheese.

She made the best cheese around. It was so creamy and salty, it'd almost melt on your tongue as soon as you tasted it.

Meanwhile, our father stood with his workers and closest friends by Tio Joca's truck. Tio Joca had parked on the opposite corner from where the street sign would be revealed. The truck's radio was on, but all one could hear was the monotone hum of my father's favorite show. He leaned against the passenger door without saying much at all, both hands tucked inside his pockets, while his drink rested on the truck step. He had cleaned up alright but couldn't be convinced to wear his nicest suit, as much as our mother had tried. Pai said it wasn't appropriate.

Whenever someone walked by with a platter, our father and his friends would help themselves with preserved hard-boiled eggs, *pastel de carne*, or more *cachaça*. Tio Joca glanced at his wristwatch and at the lowering sun, then moved on to pull out a crate from his truck, placing it underneath the street sign still covered with a black cloth.

"Antonio, *Senhor*, I think that everybody would like a speech, right?" He glanced at the crowd while approaching our father. A big smile on his face. One of his incisors was edged in gold, and sparkled against the sun's pinkish light.

Our father looked down at his polished shoes while our mother rushed to his side. Pablo and I followed her.

"Antonio," she called in a whisper. "Isn't Brizola coming? Shouldn't we wait?"

"He's not coming, Rose," our father replied. The state governor had become a friend of our father, but as it turned out, he was on the very first list the military had put out of people considered enemies of the Union, and he was gradually losing ground. What our father sensed, and we had no idea, was that Brizola had probably already fled to Uruguay by then.

"But didn't the governor say he would?" our mother insisted.

"I told you he's not coming, Rose."

Mãe stared at her white patent leather shoes for a second. Framed in mud, but still cleaner than one would expect. She

7

looked up again, at our father's eyes, but didn't say anything. Pablo and I glanced at each other wondering what could be going on with him.

"Speech, Antonio! *Vamos*, give us a speech!" Tio Joca stood by the wooden crate. Others followed his lead, making demands, while our mother seemed to try to hide her disappointment, or sadness. Pai looked at her for a moment, and walked over to Tio Joca, who was still pointing at the crate as an invitation.

"That's alright," he said, refusing to step onto the crate. My father was one of the tallest men I knew. He stood in front of it, while Tio Joca ceremoniously pulled the cover off the street sign, as if a bull was coming for it, revealing a white board with our father's name on it in blue bold capital letters. Everybody clapped, and so did our mother.

He stood there waiting for people to stop clapping. Nodding and putting both his hands out as if pleading for everybody to just quit the nonsense, which made Pablo and me clap louder.

"Well," he said against the crowd's noise, while we gradually turned silent. "*Bom*, I just wanted to thank you for this. It is very nice." He glanced at the sign again. "But, you know, there is coal here for years and years, and pretty soon people won't even remember who I was."

"*Não!*" the crowd protested. Pablo and I joined them.

"It's true, though." he insisted. "I won't be here forever. But this coal, it sure will." He smiled. "Anyway, *muito obrigado*. This is quite an honor."

And with that he walked back to Tio Joca's truck to listen to the end of his program. We all clapped again, somewhat disappointed.

...

While everything was changing in our country, Minas do Leão remained life as usual for quite some time. One main street, one church, one school, one food store, one coal mine, and one cemetery. What changed was that people would wait even more anxiously for the Sunday papers to be delivered, and those who had a TV set got used to having guests during the news broadcast as opposed to having them arrive later for the *telenovela*. At home, our father was the very first change Pablo and I witnessed. Our mother seemed more annoyed by the shifts in him than anything else; treating them as something silly and self-induced. As if he were trying to feel included in something he just was not. A few times, I heard her tell her friends that her husband had gotten his period again, and they would all laugh.

Had Mae been right, Pablo and I suffered from the same malady as our father. At night, in our rooms, we would exchange information in the dark as if it were forbidden, as if the walls had eyes and ears, and as if spies were everywhere. Pablo on the foot of my bed whispering how he had heard that a dictatorship meant you were not free; like slaves, he'd said. Me, wrapped in a blanket, crouched on the floor by his bed, repeating what Father José had said at Sunday School, that a good Catholic would not do the things our leaders were doing, that a good Catholic would not torture young people the way they did. But then when Clara had asked him why Jesus was treated the way he was, Father José had to think for a moment.

Pablo and I would watch our father, watch the way his gaze would land on a random dishcloth at dinner time and just stay there, while our mother would go on and on about the latest gossip around town. Tia Mercedes had lost her baby again, the poor thing, her fourth miscarriage; maybe if her husband would quit drinking so much *cachaça* their baby would have a better chance, something about his swimmers not being good enough swimmers. While she talked, we watched him, hoping that he was right, hoping we were in fact all included, hoping that he knew something we didn't yet know. *Oh how naïve we were!*

But once I had a better grasp of what it all meant, I began to understand why Mãe fought so hard to deny its presence in our house, to keep it out. The regime did take its time to enter

9

our lives, like the grayish green mold you'd see on the outside walls of your home, knowing that it will eventually creep into its interior. She knew. And we watched passively as things began to change.

...

In the mornings, we ate eggs with black beans and *carreteiro* and fried yucca and *murcilha* and whatever else was left over from the week. Only sometimes there would be homemade bread to go with it. Our father liked having a rich breakfast, and during the winter we liked it too. He ate with our mother and left the house before 5am each morning to go to the mine and oversee each change of shifts. He said it was important to check how much was done during the night and say goodbye to the miners, as well as greet the next group as they came down.

One of those winter mornings I woke up to the sound of steps in Pablo's room. Nothing could be seen beyond the fogged windows, as there wasn't a hint of sunlight quite yet. I followed Pablo's rushed steps across the hallway. There were no signs of anybody up, and for a moment I wondered if he could be sleepwalking. Pablo was in his pajamas. The hems of his sweatpants already way above his ankles, and his shirt barely covering his lower back. At seventeen, Pablo was almost as tall as our father. He fed the fire with two logs and one pine knot, his ribcage visible through his two-sizes-too-small old thinned-out shirt. He went to the kitchen where water was already heating up for coffee. The kitchen door was closed but unlocked, which meant that our mother must have already gone out to collect eggs.

Pablo checked on the water pot, pulled out plates and silverware, walking around as if he hadn't slept at all. He put on his beanie and opened the back door to check on our mother. He stood on the doorway and searched the backyard; his breath was a steamy cloud in front of him. Pablo and our father had built a staircase on the side of the house, and a door leading to what became our kitchen. It was supposed to be the house's back door, not meant for guests, but it was easier and it quickly became the house's main entrance.

Pablo came back inside and finished setting the table for all four of us when our mother came in, almost dropping the eggs she held in her hands when she saw us both in the kitchen. When our father walked in, already in his work boots and uniform, he too was surprised to see us up.

"*Bom dia*, boys," he said. "Did you fall off your beds this morning?"

Our mother smiled tenderly.

"I like waking up this early," Pablo said.

"Well, good for you, Pablo," our father responded, looking at Mãe.

"Eggs are almost ready, and I heated up the stew from last night." Our mother set both pans on the center of the table and invited us to sit.

"Pai," said Pablo, rather tentatively.

"What's that, *filho*?" His fork broke through the steamy potatoes.

"Can I please start working at the mine? Just the afternoon shift, when I'm back from school?"

"I told you *no* already. Not until you're done."

"But it's just six more months. I'm bored," he whined. "And besides, I want to start saving up some."

Our father dropped his fork for a moment, sipped his coffee. And looked straight into Pablo's eyes.

"It's hard work, Pablo. And you'll do enough of it. In fact, you'll get sick of that mine. Believe me." He brought another piece of meat to his plate. "And besides, you have a job. It's your school. When you're done with this job, you'll move on to the next."

"But, Pai, can't I at least start training for it?" He was tearing up.

"You want more responsibilities? You need more duties?" His voice was one degree louder than usual, but still calm enough. "Help your mother around the house. She can always use your boys' help."

Before leaving the house our father said that he was going to invite some of his friends over that evening to drink some *quentão*, and asked our mother if she could boil some. They believed the alcohol could clean their lungs of all the coal dust they breathed day in and day out. And at least twice a week our father would have some of his closest friends over for drinks - *quentão* during the winter and *cachaça* during the summer.

"How many of them tonight, *amor*?" she asked, looking at the pots she had available.

"Oh, the usual. About ten or fifteen."

By four o'clock that afternoon our mother had put the biggest pot she owned to work. The scent of boiling red wine and cloves had taken over both floors of our home. The smell of it mixed with burnt pine was enough to make us forget the cold outside. Our mother baked a large bread to go with it, all the while humming around the kitchen, as if we were celebrating something. Mãe loved to entertain, and she liked to watch our father with his friends, telling jokes like he used to tell us before the coup.

Meanwhile, to prove his point, Pablo mowed the lawn and cleaned the chicken coop. By sundown, he had also washed the entire tool shed exterior, watching as the coal-stained water slid through its white walls and fell on the coal-stained mud.

By then the smell of *quentão* was spilling through our home's windows and ceiling. Its scent, so warm and strong that people would know that she had made it even before they walked in. It was a heart-warming drink, the reason why our parents would let us have a sip or two. It was sweet too, and felt as though it multiplied inside of you, creating a hot protective layer to your bones against the unforgiving cold.

That evening I kept an eye on Mãe while Pablo sunk an old *leiteira* into the large pot of *quentão*, sneaking out the door to meet with his friends.

...

The heat deep inside his stomach all the way up to the very tip of his tongue and the roof of his mouth was nothing new to him. He had had *quentão* many many times. What was new was the tingle in his feet, the looseness on the back of his knees and neck, and just how bright and blurry a starry night could be.

Eduardo had brought a bottle of *cachaça* with him, and between him and Pablo and Rita and Jerônimo, they were almost through all the alcohol they had. Pablo leaned against a tree, his feet planted in the meadow as if hoping to mirror his solid companion. Jerônimo, always the clown, was clumsily dancing *chula*, a squatting, tap-dance mess. Rita immediately joined in, smiling, slightly uncoordinated, but nothing short of pure grace. She'd steal glances at Pablo's eyes as often as she could hold her focus. The both of them danced for a short while, Eduardo clapped and laughed hysterically. Pablo just watched her, mesmerized.

When they stopped, she walked over to him, and gave him a long, wet kiss. This was also new to him. She kissed differently, and she tasted differently as if she had suddenly, in one kiss, revealed to him the woman she would become. Somewhat startled, Pablo opened his eyes to look at his friends, but both of them had their backs to the couple, and were watching the lights on the mine twinkle behind the trees that stood between them.

Rita stopped kissing him. Grabbed his face with both hands, and said, "I really like you, Pablo Fonte, did you know that?"

Pablo tightened his grip around her waist, pulling her closer to him. Then he kissed her again, wondering if his kisses were as telling as hers, and how far he was from becoming this man he hoped to be. And that's the last memory he had of that evening.

TWO

MÃE HAD ASKED me to fetch some parsley from our backyard, and I when got out I noticed Pablo standing next to the shed; his saw hung from his right hand as his left shielded his eyes from the setting sun. He stretched his neck as if to make sense of what could be going on at the mine. We lived about a half a mile from the mine, the closest house to it, close enough to hear the quietest of explosions, or see when the trucks pulled in or out for coal.

"Pablo!" I called, but he didn't look at me. "Pablo! What?"

"Something going on at the mine. Saw a bunch of cars pulling up." His eyes were fixed on the horizon.

"Probably visitors. Pai said there's a new mine in Butiá. He's probably teaching them a thing or two." The air was crisp enough to cut through one's nostrils.

"Yeah. I don't know." He leaned his saw against the shed's door. "I'm gonna go peek," he announced and immediately started running. "Tell Mãe that I'll come back with Pai."

"Wait! I want to go!" But he didn't look back.

...

Pablo crawled between trees, bushes and some of the cars in an effort to inch himself closer to where all the men stood. No sound came out of the mine. No trucks pulled in or out. No workers rested by its entrance, no stray dogs feasted on leftovers. It was all silence.

Pablo's knees dug the black wet mud, and he thought of our mother, and how upset she'd be once she saw how careless he had been with his clothing. His heart was almost jumping out of his chest from the sprint, and his stomach suddenly felt empty, as if a winter wind ran through him, taking away everything that was familiar, and replacing it with the new folds of life, the inevitable changes revealing themselves right in front of you, and inside of you. Pablo spotted a few pink wood sorrels close by, their petals shutting in on themselves as they prepared for a long frosty night. He plucked five or six of them and started to munch at their crunchy stems, hoping the tart juices would tame the storm within his stomach.

While savoring the *azedinhas*, Pablo monitored three men armed with rifles pacing across the mine's main entrance, right by the elevator shaft. Two of them exchanged small talk, while the third, the taller one, paid close attention to José, the security guard on duty.

José had monitored the afternoon shift ever since people started mining that place. He was a quiet man who knew all there was to know about what happened in that mine. He spotted the army convoy as the first car turned the street corner, almost a kilometer away, and immediately called our father by cranking the telephone as fast as he could. José knew he was being watched, and stood still.

The guards' hardhats didn't look much different from those worn inside the mine, but everything else about them seemed foreign and dangerous. That was the first time that my brother had seen their boots and uniforms up close and thought it a lot more intimidating than he'd expected. Pablo reached for some rocks underneath him, saving them inside his pockets for a few seconds, but returned them to where they belonged as soon as he got another look at the men's rifles. The temperature was dropping quite fast, and in his impulse and curiosity he'd forgotten his coat inside the shed. His lips hardened as they assumed a dark tint of red and purple. His fingers felt the chill as well, and he breathed into his cupped hand to ease the pain. A cloud of his breath hung in the air. It seemed everything hung in the air. Pablo glanced at his other hand as he pressed it against the damp coal-tainted mud as if lulling it into revealing its secrets, into sharing whatever was going on within its caves.

While my brother waited, our father stood inside, hand

holding hand behind his back. His men lined up behind him, like little wary children, sharing stares between him, the army and each other, as they allowed our father to ponder the choices offered by the General. Some of the miners posed as if they were about to have their portrait taken, hoping their faces, their already nostalgic eyes would tell each of their stories for generations to come. Some held on to their tools as if they were mementos they should never part with, while others hooked their thumbs through their belt loops, on a desperate attempt to look tough. After a day's work inside the mine, the men were covered in black dust, creating the illusion of a uniformed army, or that of slaves, depending on who was watching.

Pai looked at nothing but one wall of the galleria where they all stood. Through the carbide lamps hanging from some of the wood planks, he saw the tunnel his own hands had helped carve, and thought of his two boys. He saw the image of Pablo and me running through the passages with oversized hardhats. He saw us zipping past him inside a wagon as one of his workers, one of his friends, pushed us as fast as he possibly could. He heard the silly sound of my laughter when I tried to contain myself, and Pablo's shushing, hoping we weren't too much of a disruption.

Our father turned his right foot from side to side as if to smooth the surface underneath him, but really just trying to remind himself of how the earth below the earth felt soothing and familiar against his work shoes. That gravel, the stench of sulfur almost like vinegar, the blackness on his men's faces, the wood planks, the maze… All these things he thought he knew better than the back of his own wife's hands. He was a little older than Pablo when he became a miner and never thought he'd have a different life. And as he contemplated his years inside the mine, he wondered whether he could work for the government, and more importantly, if he could heed a man he despised.

He took his hat off and looked at each of his men's faces. With their eyes wide open, they followed his every movement hoping that he would take the offer and continue to be the person they looked up to, continue to be the man they came for when their son had caught the flu and they needed an advance for the antibiotics, or when their in-law had passed and they needed a day off for the wake. The General who had made the offer grew impatient as our father took his time. His thick and bushy eyebrows arched inward in a frown as he caught a glimpse of his own subordinates' unrest, exchanging quizzical looks with one another.

What the General didn't mention in his offer was that he also expected our father to be the man who'd report back to him, who would tell on his own friends when anybody went astray, when anybody dared to criticize the changes pushed upon them. He would be the one to fire workers for causes with which he wouldn't necessarily agree. He would be the person who would have to turn somebody in when he was probably the one who despised the whole thing more than anybody else. No. The General didn't mention any of that. But our father knew, and his men had a feeling.

"General." His last name was Machado, as I would later find out. "I would like to respectfully decline your offer, Sir." One could clearly see the lament on his men's faces, the whites of their eyes one by one disappearing behind their eyelids as each man turned inward. They too had a decision to make.

Our father took one last look at each of his workers and watched the weight of what he had said sink in. Some of them took their hardhats off like their boss had done and held it by their stomach, as one would do when entering a church on a Sunday morning. Showing the same respect and sadness for the inevitable distance one was bound to have with anything holy like god himself or, in that case, the mine, its miners and their guardian Santa Barbara.

The General clicked his tongue annoyed at our father's audacity, "Guess you better go home and tell your family they need to provide for themselves from now on." He wore a smirk on his face, which our father didn't see because he was studying the mine.

As he continued to take it all in, he said quietly, but loud enough for those closer to him, including the General himself, to hear "With all due respect, Sir, my family is my own problem."

"If there's anybody else here who wants to be dumb like Mr. Fonte, please do so now. I have no patience for those who won't commit to the Union."

Out of the fifty workers on that shift, in that section of the mine, about fifteen stepped forward and left with our father without saying a word to the General. Each of them stopped by Santa Barbara's statue on their way out to ask for her blessing one last time.

Outside, Pablo suddenly saw the three soldiers shuffle by the entrance as they noticed the crowd coming towards them. José didn't move. The sun had already set, but its light still infused the open meadow. Our father nodded to one of the soldiers as he walked past them.

"You're going to die of hunger, old man."

"And you of guilt, kid," our father said, bringing a smile to Pablo's face.

Pablo would repeat this dialogue to me over and over, his eyes never failing to sparkle with pride. He watched our father leave the mine without really knowing what was going on. Although he couldn't ignore the way his shoulders hunched forward as Pai watched the gravel disappear underneath his feet.

Pablo was aware this was one of the moments when life did the living despite one's will. He stayed where he was, pushing his knuckles against the chilly mud as if punishing it for allowing itself to be taken away from all of us. He thought of the dark coal below, of the murky mud, of nature's darkest wonders, and how much he wanted to be tough and wondrous just like it. But Pablo was all cotton – volatile, weightless, and easily tainted.

. . .

The mine remained open for only a few weeks before they shut it all down due to the lack of workforce. When it happened, people hoped things would go back to normal once again, that they couldn't sustain it, and that our father would soon be called to resume his position. But two months went by and nobody heard a thing. The mine became a mix of a ghost town and an amusement park. Despite the scary stories going around, kids would eventually find their way back into its caves, zipping along the galleries while playing hide-and-seek, sharing ghost stories, or playing *jogo do copo*, hoping the spirits would reveal what lied ahead for each of them, or who would win the *Brasileirão* that year.

One day Clara, Xico and I were bored and decided to see if there was anybody playing in the mine. But when we got to the very first galleria we saw a couple kissing.

"Shush!" whispered Xico.

Clara looked at me with a big smile as we walked towards them. I looked back at the couple. The guy was leaning against the wall, his legs spread apart enough for the girl to fit right in between them. She had both her hands on his head caressing his hair gently, while his hands rested on her lower back.

"Uuhh!" yelled Xico.

Rita quickly stepped back, and Pablo wiped his lips. Rita was red with embarrassment, while Pablo seemed to glow with pride.

"What are you kids doing here?" he asked. "You shouldn't be here, Luca. It's not safe."

Pablo suddenly looked so much older. As if the age gap between us had widened by at least five years, as if that kiss showed me we had nothing more in common, that we wouldn't ever play hide-and-seek in the mine again, or soccer, or just talk in the dark at night.

"You know what's not safe? What you two were about to do before we got here!" Xico said, maliciously.

"Shut up, *pia*! What do you know!?"

"C'mon, guys, let's go. Leave them alone," I said as I started to walk back.

Pablo smiled, like you would once your dog first learned a trick you've been trying to teach for a long time. Clara seemed stunned, petrified. She watched as Rita tried to hide her face behind her long hair. I grabbed her arm and walked her out.

"You two behave yourselves, huh! Or I'll have to tell your parents what you're up to!" Xico again.

"Get out, Xico. We'll talk later." Threatened Pablo.

"Maybe we should go, too," said Rita.

. . .

Pablo and I had heard on the radio that there was supposed to be a meteor shower visible in the south of Brasil. Neither of us knew what to expect, but Pablo somehow convinced our mother to let us invite our friends for a sleepover to watch it all together. It was a school night and it meant skipping the next day, as the shower wasn't supposed to hit until 3am. But saying 'no' to Pablo was never an easy quest, so he and I invited Rita, Clara, Xico, and Xico's older brother Marcos, and we all camped downstairs.

Pablo and Rita set the fire and spent most of the time talking to each other, laughing and watching the flames dance for them. Pablo played with Rita's toes while she talked; their cheeks red with heat. Clara, Xico, Marcos and I took turns playing *Damas* and *Cinco Marias*. Marcos's age was sort of in between Pablo's and mine, and it seemed to leave him conflicted as to where he stood in our little social circle. Every now and then Rita and Pablo would go out to the yard, and Marcos would just watch them like a house cat does when its owners take the dog for a walk, trying to understand why he was never included in their daily outings while also maintaining the hope that he was better off in the warm cozy house, with its toys and soft pillows.

"You should go," said Xico to his brother.

"What do you know?!" said Marcos.

"*Sim*, go ahead and bark at me. I know you're lame as hell is what I know."

"Shut up, *piá*." Marcos got up and headed for the door.

Xico shook his head from side to side.

"Just let him be, Xico," said Clara after Marcos had shut the door behind him.

"What a loser," he whispered.

"Like you're any different," she said, carefully piling up the little cloth bags. Xico went toward the fireplace.

We ate sandwiches we made ourselves downstairs. Mãe had bought a liter of Cola at the store, and made *chimarrão* to help us stay awake. While we ate, we gathered as close to the fire as we could. Pablo and Rita had told us they had a plan, and we were waiting to hear it. Pablo had found a piece of tarp large enough for us to lay in, and at 2:50 sharp, we'd go out to our backyard, taking all the blankets, pillows, jackets, scarves, gloves and whatever else we could to keep us warm while we waited.

"How about we make another fire?" asked Xico.

"How about *you* make another fire?! Right now! And keep feeding it until it's time for us to go out!" Marcos glared at his brother.

"I don't think a fire is a good idea," said Pablo, looking at Xico. "The darkest our surroundings, the better the view is what I heard. Apparently big cities can't see it that well."

We got through everything we had in front of us down to the very last slice of salami and bread crust, while we wondered what these meteors would look like.

"Just like shooting stars, I think," said Clara. "Isn't that what they are anyway?"

"I don't know. Is it? I thought it was different," I said.

"Does that mean we get to make a wish for every one we see?" Rita asked Pablo.

"*Claro!*" he said, with a smile. "Doesn't mean they'll come true, though." Rita laughed and slapped his shoulder.

Rita and Clara shared the large mattress, and us boys laid

blankets folded in half as close to the fire as we could. Pablo laid his by Rita's side, and the two of them whispered stories to each other, while we played Clara's favorite game, where somebody would give us one word, and the first to sing any song with it would win.

When Pablo's alarm went off, we were all in such deep sleep that for a few seconds it felt as though we were in a sort fire-colored-collective-nightmare. Rita mumbled something and turned her back to the fire. Xico and his brother looked even more alike than usual; their mouths wide open, belly up, knees bent and arms behind their heads. Pablo looked at me as if daring to go out when everybody else wouldn't, but I already had my gloves and cap on, and the two blankets in hand.

Both Pablo and I got sick after that night. The meteor shower would have been underwhelming to most experienced watchers, more like two or three shooting stars. But for us, it felt magical. Shooting stars on a time clock! Pablo, who had teased Rita earlier, was encouraging me to wish that we could stay in Minas forever. He'd shut his eyes for a moment then look at me to make sure I had done the same.

...

With three more months until the end of the school year, Pablo saw it as his duty to convince our parents to stay in Minas do Leão, but at dinnertime, all our father talked about was soccer matches, movie theaters, about the things he had heard college kids did for fun. The parties they would go to, the concerts they had on campus, the opportunities he would get. Nothing seemed to affect Pablo. He wanted to stay, he wanted our father's job. Once in an act of desperation Pai told Pablo something along the lines of, "Not to mention the girls, son. They just take better care of themselves in the city."

To which our mother responded, "Thank you, Antonio. That is very worldly of you. You should fit right in in this big city. A gentleman really." She walked out to tend to the garden.

Mãe didn't look at our father for a few days after that. She would feed him and clean after him. She would offer to trim his hair or pluck lint out of his clothes. She would do everything she always did, except look at him. For those days, Pai's hunched back was even more hunched over in the hopes of meeting her gaze. But Mãe seemed determined. Pablo confided in me one night how much he was enjoying their argument. Hoping that our mother's resentment could steer all of our lives in the right direction.

"When do you leave?"

Clara stood on top of a high branch, holding on to another above her head. That was her favorite avocado tree, and she knew it like her own home. I had sat on a little nook and was watching two *gaivotas* glide eastward.

"Once school is over," I said.

"Do you know where you'll live?"

I shrugged. "Pai has been looking. I don't know. I don't care."

She had hooked her legs around the branch and was hanging upside down.

"Do you want to go?" Her blond hair hung and swayed with the breeze.

I shrugged again.

"I think I'm going for the guava," I said.

"*Tá bom*. I'll be right there."

Clara's family was preparing to move, too. But they were going to Caxias do Sul, where the rest of her family was. She said she already had a few friends there. Most people were moving, as there wasn't much of a choice. A small section of the mine had reopened. And those workers who had chosen to stay had their jobs back. But the people who stayed in town, those who still spent their days inside the mine, avoided being seen with someone like our father, and at times it seemed as though they avoided being seen with any one of us.

Our mother and I saw Pablo and my father become different people, more distant and quiet. I didn't mind my father's distance that much. It was Pablo's that bothered the most. For those last three months I tried my best to compensate for their absence. Mãe continued to make quentão for the remaining cold days, hoping that old friends would stop by after a long day of work to catch up with my father. That was her way of fighting the changes around her. She'd insist on using the same bigger pot, as if any day, ten, fifteen men would show up, and that she wouldn't risk embarrassing herself and her husband by not having enough to quench everyone's thirst. No one ever came, and eventually she stopped.

Neighbors made themselves clear through small gestures that it wasn't that they didn't agree with my father's attitude but were afraid of what could happen. Assembly of any kind raised suspicions in a town like ours, and people lived within the confines of their own lives. Every once in a while, a neighbor would knock on our door with a little bit of food, saying things like "Oh, dear, I can't help but cook too much. We're used to having people over." Then the conversation would move on and both parties would lament the changes that had come and speak nostalgically about the old days. At first I thought they saw we weren't doing well without my father's pay and used this as an excuse for their charity. But as we all became more isolated, I realized they were being honest and actually looked forward to this food exchange.

Tia Mercedes was the only constant visitor. She was about our mother's age and had finally gotten pregnant after six years of trying. The whole town got involved in her and her husband's problem. Everyone prayed for them and services were held so that they would be blessed with a child. Some prayed to Jesus while others called on their *orixás* to remove whatever *macumba* was done against poor Tia Mercedes. Most people did both.

Before the coup, I remember that sometimes, in the dark of

the night, a group would gather by the creek right behind Tia Mercedes's house to "work" on her. I was intrigued by the ritual. She would stand barefooted by the creek, while people dressed in white and yellow, Oxum's colors, kneeling before her, singing, calling and waiting for Mamãe Oxum to manifest herself in one of them. We would know whoever was the chosen one because they would dance around her, speaking in tongues, as soon as Mother Oxum took possession of their body. Mamãe Oxum would hold onto Tia Mercedes's head at first and work her way down, spending more time on her belly. Then she'd continue on to the very tip of her toes, as if sending out to the water all the bad spirits, the venom within her that killed every baby before they could even have a fighting chance, demanding that the current take them, as far as they would go. Meanwhile all the others clapped and sang praises to Mamãe Oxum. But sometimes people said it wasn't Oxum who had come but some other *caboclo*. They would know it immediately because of its raspy voice and his immediate request for a *cachaça* and a cigar. They would always have them handy in case the *caboclo* showed up, as to not upset him.

I never quite understood Umbanda and its orixás. But whatever they did, it had worked in time. A meeting in the dark like this would not sit well after the coup. But now Tia Mercedes was very much pregnant, and this couple's only trouble was that her husband had left the mine with our father and was also out of a job.

Their similar situation had brought Tia Mercedes and our mother very close. There wasn't one afternoon that she didn't stop by to chat. She'd stand by the kitchen door, caressing her enormous belly, while watching our mother work. It was surprising to me that they got along. Our mother was in a constant state of denial, it seemed. Telling people left and right that everything was fine, that her husband had all sorts of opportunities now that he was no longer buried in that mine, that Pablo was happy to be going to college next year, and that age meant nothing to me, whatever that meant.

While my mother created her alternate perfect universe, Tia couldn't bring herself to look away from her reality. She did everything she could to convince her husband they should move. But he was hardheaded. A man of the *pampas*, he'd say. Not meant for the big city. In all her fears and no matter how frustrated she was that her husband refused to see the trouble they were in, somehow she kept coming back. Somehow listening to our mother's optimistic, if not delirious, stories seemed to soothe her and her unborn baby. Mãe must have been her afternoon escape.

. . .

As we reached the final days of October, our mother began to gradually repopulate our first floor. She opened it all up and decorated it with more flowers than usual, hoping the spring air would blossom life back into that house. Tia Mercedes would often bring flowers she had picked up along the way, and would watch as Mãe turned them into what she considered perfect arrangements. She would spend entire afternoons as our mother worked in the kitchen, baking bread, roasting beef, cooking rice, squeezing fresh fruit into juice, and chopping every single kind of fruit she could get her hands on into a fruit salad. She'd place a huge bowl on the center of the table, arranging it so every single fruit would be fairly featured. She'd stand over the table, tilting her head to the side just a little while pondering whether the arrangement was good enough.

"It's gorgeous, Rose!" Tia Mercedes would always say.

Every single day became an event as my mother worked tirelessly to set up family meals downstairs. Her low heels echoed against the steps as she transferred everything downstairs then brought it back up again.

"I'm driving to the city tomorrow, Rose," our father

announced one evening while our mother served us fruit salad in a silver chalice.

That was another change. We stopped using our daily dishes and silverware since what had happened at the mine. My mother wasn't willing to wait for special occasions.

"Uhum." She picked a few grapes from the bowl, placing them carefully in the chalice, by the honeydew. Our father would go to Porto Alegre every week in search of a home for us, of a job, and of space. Every once in a while he'd invite her.

"There are two houses I was hoping you'd see. I think you'll like them, Rosey. They both have decent sized backyards; we could plant a few vegetables." He watched her.

"Oh, honey, there's just too much to do around the house. I promise you I'll be fine with whatever you choose. I trust you." She brought her chalice closer to her and was aimlessly moving pieces around with her fork. "Besides, I don't think I want to see it beforehand. I might as well just see it when it's time." She tried a smile.

Pablo shuffled in his seat as he finished his meal. His hair was growing longer, and our mother had stopped bothering him to let her cut it.

"Do you want to come with me, Pablo?"

"Nah," he replied. "I have a paper due on Friday."

"How about you, Luca?"

He seemed exhausted from the amount of effort it took to act normal and talk through a meal.

"Sorry, Pai, I have a lot of homework." He nodded as if he already knew what my answer would be. "Maybe next time?"

"Sure." He finished his juice. "Now, will you excuse me?"

We all nodded, and my mother watched him go. It was a clear night outside, and through the windows we could hear the frogs and crickets singing their laments as the breeze announced the coming rain. I thought about how it had been a while since we all had a conversation. I looked at my father and wondered whether conversations would gradually feel more and more artificial. I wondered if our lives had become a desperate attempt to hold on to the memories of people who no longer existed. And if we could ever be content with whom we had become.

My father washed his hands and mouth in the kitchen sink; age seemed to catch up to him a lot faster since he stopped working. Pai seemed hopeless, as his mind fueled his body's decay. Our mother, on the other hand, behaved as if she was all hope.

For the most part, I thought Pablo and my father didn't notice how much our mother needed them to just be present for one moment, to actually look at her. One decent conversation was all it took to lighten up her day. One small meaningless exchange of words, and she'd put on a hopeful smile across her face and a twinkle in her hazel eyes. I would rarely go outside so that I could help her with her chores, and show her that I hadn't changed, that she didn't need to worry about me. It became my job to stay the same, and at times I felt it a burden. It took me years to realize how I was doing all that for myself and not my mother; how I was the one desperately counting on her to stay exactly the same.

THREE

WHEN HE ARRIVED in Porto Alegre that day, he didn't hesitate on which streets to take, or which stop signs to ignore. The city was gradually becoming something familiar to him. He had been studying its paths with the similar intent he had devoted to the mine and its caves his whole life. My father created maps in his head. Maps of places, of people and the way they behaved. He was comforted by the illusion that he could tell how someone would react before that person even knew it. This would soon be the reason everybody around him became a disappointment.

He drove slowly past some of the taller buildings, watching them carefully as he waited for pedestrians to cross the street at a busy corner. People were everywhere, and they walked fanning themselves with their hands, a piece of paper, a notebook, anything. My father unbuttoned the collar of his shirt and loosened his tie just a little. He rolled down the car window and put his elbow out as he made his way to the back streets where he would reach a house he wanted to look at. *Um formigueiro*, was what he thought downtown Porto Alegre looked like. Given the vastness of the country, how could there be that many people in just one place?

When he was finally able to get through the crowds, he drove across Rua Duque de Caxias by the cathedral and went downhill until he turned right on Rua do Arvoredo, a small, quiet cobblestone street, strategically positioned between the city's main church and its cemetery. One of the few homes with some land left downtown.

He had already seen this house's interior with the broker the last time he'd been to the city. But he'd decided to go back and look at its exterior yet again; its windows, what you could see from the veranda, what the earth in the front yard felt like on the tip of your fingers, what kinds of birds stopped by, and what songs they sang. He parked his car across the street. On the sidewalk sat a pile of trash bags waiting for collection, and he wondered which days of the week he would hear the trash truck drive by, how long it took for the pack of dogs to bark at the workers. He slowly made his way across the cobblestones to the house's front gate. The gate was closed but one could easily open the latch. He walked up the steps to the front porch, pushing his foot down with each step to test the wood's condition. It seemed firm enough.

He thought about going around the house, checking its windows, finding out whatever flaws were exposed, but instead he took a seat on the top step and watched the road for a while. He wanted to learn about the type of people who would walk by, the noises his wife would hear, and the speed with which cars would drive through this street. He could hear the traffic coming from everywhere. Honks, cars coming to a full stop, buses and trucks picking up speed. It wasn't loud, but it was a constant reminder that being there made you part of something much bigger than what we were used to.

He suddenly felt a light breeze kiss the back of his ear and swipe across his shoulders and he imagined it travelling all the way from Rio Guaíba to this house. To him. And that made him feel somewhat connected to this place. He was beginning to understand the way it existed with nature, the way it existed with this city, and the way it could exist once we were in it. He picked up an *azedinha*, and while munching on its stem, he looked back at the front window and pictured the living room he had seen not too long ago. He imagined my mother's flower arrangements giving life to the place. He pictured himself sitting in that same living room, pulling up a chair to the window to listen to his radio while watching the life outside. He stared at that shut window for a while, then got up to make sure you could really lock it.

Finally, my father walked through the front yard, searching for anything that had survived the long months of neglect since the house had been vacant. There was nothing but weeds and one tangerine tree. He dug his fingers into the earth and scooped out a small amount which he brought up to his nose. It smelled of life. Of new life. He smiled and rubbed his hands together with that earth in between as it slowly fell back to the ground. It was as close to black as his hands would get from then on. This was his new coal. He suddenly saw his wife's garden blooming there. He saw her sitting on the porch, knitting, while that same gentle breeze brushed her light brown hair. He saw Pablo and me playing soccer out on the street. My father had made his decision.

. . .

Pablo would disappear for whole days, meeting up with Rita or his friends after school. When he was around, he was so quiet that he might as well have not been there at all. Our mother didn't mind his silence as long as he sat with us for supper.

One day, Mãe asked me to feed a chicken we kept separate from all the others to make a broth for Tia Mercedes, who had stopped coming to our house now that her baby was about to be born. Our mother had insisted Tia Mercedes should rest, and she listened. It was customary for neighbors to feed a new mother with the 'cleanest' bird in an effort to strengthen her body and her milk after going through labor.

It was late in the afternoon. The clouds could be so thick and low some days that one couldn't even trace the sun behind them. It created a stillness in the air that almost felt as if we all lived inside an opaque bubble, where every sound and every smell lingered around us. I smelled tobacco and wondered if our father had taken up smoking again. He'd quit not long ago, after spending a whole month in bed with a cough that just wouldn't let go of him.

I followed the smell quietly, knowing how loud things were on days like those. Pablo sat on the grass with his back against the rear wall of the tool shed. He watched the stillness in the mine. His eyes brooded across the meadow we used to play, over the mine and the horizon. I then saw a little spark and realized that a cigarette hung from the corner of his mouth. He took a drag, then held the cigarette between his thumb and forefinger, the same way our father would do, while he contemplated the shapes he created with the smoke coming out of his mouth. I didn't know that he smoked, but I wasn't surprised. I thought about going up to him, about asking him what the hell he was doing, but since he didn't notice me I figured it was best to just let him be.

Later that evening, I watched the rain run down the windowpane as I waited for our mother to call us at dinnertime. I wanted to cry, to seek some kind of release from all the fears I had, from this new life and this new family I sometimes felt stuck with. And just like that I became aware for the very first time of one's loneliness. The entire concept of family suddenly seemed like nothing more than an illusion. In the end we were all alone. I craved my brother's company. I needed him to explain things to me, all the things I could not know. And I resented his absence, his selfishness.

I put the downstairs mattress right by the window and lay down on it, staring at the water, gradually washing away the coal dust that couldn't have been there for more than two days. I traced the fading gray streaks and listened to the sound of that tainted water hitting the earth. I imagined it gliding above the mud and slipping below our home, finding its own temporary home there, so that one dry windy day it could be swept up in between the wood planks of our floor for us to breathe it all over again. I folded my arms, resting my nape on top of my trembling hands, and crossed my legs as if I was a miner about to nap in a quiet cave. All the while pretending that life wasn't scary, that I wasn't afraid, because that was what I thought men did. That was what I thought that men should do.

. . .

We left Minas do Leão two days after Pablo's graduation. The sun succumbed behind dense clouds, heavy with rain, threatening to release themselves on most of our furniture as we loaded Tio Joca's truck with the few things our parents had decided on taking with us. We were mostly quiet. All we heard were the thumps and clacks and bangs of our belongings hitting the floor of Tio Joca's dirty truck, while its radio hummed a highly inflected, almost theatrical speech, what I had begun to associate with political propaganda.

As we got through the morning, a few neighbors stopped by to say their farewells. They would wish us luck, and that God would guide us. Some would lament our departure, clasping their hands together, tilting their heads to the side or simply staring at the black dirt beneath us. But we knew my father had become a liability, and deep down they all must have felt great relief in seeing him go. Whenever someone came with a sad face, or a farewell gift, I went inside the house pretending to focus on the boxes, but eventually my name would be called, and I would have to show my face, my smiling and polite face, and say goodbye, and thank them for whatever it was that I had to thank them for.

As we were getting ready to leave, Pablo and I went around the house taking one last look at its empty rooms, silently saying our goodbyes. While I was still inside, Pablo had hid himself behind the shed once again. I found him kneeling down, and kissing the ground that stretched all the way to the mine. Pablo lit a cigarette and studied its quietness, while the cigarette burnt itself up to the filter. I walked up to him after I said goodbye to our chickens, that Tia Mercedes would keep, and Xuxa the stray dog I had adopted a couple months prior, when our parents didn't care enough to say 'no'. Xuxa didn't like being petted all that much, but she enjoyed my company. She'd follow me around like a younger sister, watching my every move. I wondered what would happen to her. Xuxa was lucky that she got to stay, that she got to have such independent life.

When I went up to Pablo, it was as if my presence reminded him of how tough he had to be. He squinted as he looked at me, and took a long drag of his so far ignored cigarette.

"Big city, huh?" he offered.

"*É.*"

While Pablo took his time in the backyard, saying goodbye to the piece of land where we had always played, the shed, the meadow and its smells, our mother took some time inside the house. I could hear her clogs slowly thumping against the wood floor. I saw her through the kitchen window, staring at the vastness outside. Meanwhile, our father waited for us in the car.

We followed Tio Joca's truck. Our father and Pablo took one last glimpse at the mine as we headed down the main road, without saying a word. Our mother gently caressed the rabbit foot she held in between her fingers with one hand, while bringing her golden São Jorge necklace pendant to her lips with her other. She kissed it gently. Her eyes shut.

The rain never came, much to our mother's disappointment. She had spent the entire morning saying that a big heavy rain would be a blessing when anybody showed signs of concern for our furniture. She made herself believe the rain would clear everything out from bad spirits, negative energy, karma, whatever it was that shook people out of synch in their lives. And when we didn't see a drop of water hit the windshield, I realized that my mother feared that the change of houses, of schools, of cities, was all for nothing. That regardless of where we were, the ghosts of who we used to be would be with us. Quiet. Dormant. Like uninvited guests.

Our father held firmly onto the steering wheel, looking straight ahead, without so much as glancing at the farms on the side of the road. He seemed relieved or hopeful to have succeeded in leaving that town and its mine behind. If anything, he looked determined. He watched our belongings sticking up from the truck, bouncing with the road's unevenness, as though certain of a brighter beginning.

Pablo and my mother observed the side of the road, the scenery they knew so well, refusing to look ahead. They paid attention to every cow lying around, to every yucca plantation, to every strawberry farm. They watched some of the people who walked alongside of the road with a hint of jealousy in their eyes. Every once in a while my mother would remember to gently caress her São Jorge, hanging over her chest. Our father turned the dial on the stereo, while we all stared at his hand hoping that something would magically play itself. Any cheap melody to save us from ourselves. But nothing. None of the radio stations worked.

It was mid-afternoon when we arrived, and the same thick clouds had followed us, covering the top of some of the city's higher buildings. Pablo watched the commercial buildings go by, and streetlights change colors, and billboards announce movie premieres, cleaning products and beer.

The city seemed chaotic at first, but it wasn't at all. Everything and everybody seemed to have a purpose, more so than where we lived. People were everywhere. There were more pedestrians in one block than habitants in the entire Minas do Leão. They spilled out from the sidewalks, taking over the edge of the roads. They walked in between the cars that waited on a red light. Our father didn't hesitate despite the traffic. It was clear he knew the rules and knew where he was going. Our mother, next to him, looked as if she wasn't there at all.

We pulled up to a one-story house, the second from the corner. It looked plain with its white stucco and dark brown windows. The front yard could have used some work, but it wasn't bad. My mother watched it carefully, probably wondering which flowers she'd want blooming there in a few months. An iron fence circled the property. It was plain and not very tall, standing level to my twelve-year-old chest.

"This is it!" our father announced. He walked up the steps

of the front porch and looked at our mother who still studied the garden.

"There's a nice breeze here, Rose," he said. He spread his arms to cover both sides of the porch. "I think you'll enjoy sitting here to do your knitting."

"I'm sure I will," she said. "The house is lovely, dear."

My father let a childish smile escape him, and we all went inside. In the living room sat a deep avocado-green rotary-dial phone. Pai pointed at it with the same excitement he'd shown before.

"Rose?" he called. "What do you think?"

It was our very first telephone. Whenever necessary, we'd use the mine's. Our mother smiled at the gadget sitting by the fireplace mantel.

"That way you can stay in touch when Mercedes' baby is born, or with whoever you want."

"Wonderful, Antonio. Thank you," she said while he gently kissed her forehead.

Pablo and I picked our rooms without much of a fuss. I kept the room between Pablo's and my parents'. It was smaller but closer to the bathroom. I stood in the hallway that led to all of the bedrooms and looked for any signs of an incline. There was nothing. I wondered if given enough time, if this house would also become slanted. If it would ever feel as though it was ours. I remember thinking that a leveled house would probably be a good thing at that point. I was too old to play with marbles anyway.

. . .

Inside the mine is quiet. I walk by myself through the empty gallerias, and they look darker than I remember. Darker and vaster. There isn't a worker in sight, but several abandoned wagons; some half-full, others empty. It's all just sitting there, forgotten. I must have broken into it. I'm looking for something, or for someone. The mine's paths are not as clear when nobody is working it. I must be looking for Pablo. I'm always looking for Pablo. I see one wall in the galleria to my right lighten up in a fading, almost imperceptible orange color. The light shifts around. I walk towards it and sense the smell of sulfur being overtaken by another smell. It's tobacco. I must have found Pablo. Why does he insist on smoking? I keep my slow pace and study the light's patterns. It moves up every once in a while, but it mostly illuminates the ground and lower sections of the walls.

My breathing weakens as I walk. Shorter breaths, as if my lungs are being consumed by poison. With his body leaning against the opposite side, I find Pablo staring at a wall, his right foot pressed against it as if he's studying the horizon, as if he's studying something beautiful. But there is no horizon. It's just a black wall he'd seen many times. He looks as though he was expecting me, but he doesn't notice that I'm standing right there.

I touch the rough surface with my right hand. My hand isn't mine. It looks more like Pablo's; wider and stronger.

"What are you doing here?" As the words come out of my mouth, I sense a kind of burnt wood taste rising in my throat, all the way to the insides of my cheeks and the tip of my tongue. I smell the cigarette smoke coming out of me. A dense cloud hangs in the air, and I can barely make up Pablo's figure.

"What are you talking about?" My mouth makes up the words coming out of his mouth. He sounds like me. Or I sound like him.

"Why are you smoking?" That strange taste again. Another cloud forms in front of my face, my view of Pablo polluted.

"I'm not." He's smiling a smile I don't recognize. Wicked almost.

FOUR

I LONGED TO go outside like we used to back home. I missed going to the mine, watching our father work, and trying on hardhats with a bit of *carbureto* left in their little containers. Pablo and I would collect all the saliva we could manage and spit into these containers to light them up real bright. Then we would find the darkest and emptiest galleria around, and pretend our light beams were swords, and just bobble our heads around to put on a good fight. We mostly just laughed at each other. Our father wouldn't let us stay there for too long, though. He said the stench had to be bad for our lungs, and he was right as it turned out. Pablo and I always tried to keep as quiet as possible in hopes that he would forget we were still in there.

The longer we stayed inside the mine, the more blinding the sun could be once we made our way out of its tunnels. Pablo had our mother's hazel eyes, which were more sensitive to the light than mine. It would take him a good five minutes to actually see straight. And I loved pointing at obstacles that didn't really exist, just to trick him. Sometimes he would get back at me by pretending that he wasn't seeing clearly and purposely bump into me, or ask me to guide him. He would hook his hand around my arm, and pull me downward, tripping on my foot, making us both lose our balance and fall, then just laugh in my face in the end.

...

We had only been in Porto Alegre for about six months. Winter had proven itself just as unforgiving as the ones back home, and one afternoon Pablo walked into my room, with the thickest jacket he had, and the last scarf and beanie our mother had knitted for him. I was sitting on the parquet floor with my homework spread across my bed, and Pablo went straight for my wardrobe, grabbing my navy coat.

"Are you done with your homework yet? I want to take you somewhere," he said. Pablo's face was changing. At almost eighteen, he had no fat on his face at all; his cheeks were hollow concaves shadowed only by his protruding cheekbones, making him look a lot older than me, a lot older than he actually was. And when he smiled, you could see the places where he would have had lines around his eyes and where his cheeks would've been vertically marked by age. He had the kind of smile where people seem to be smiling at something but are actually thinking of something else. As if he knew something you couldn't possibly know, as if he was in control of all the things there were for me to know, and I depended on his good will to share them with me. For most of his life, he did.

I jumped up and dropped my pencil, which fell on my math book and rolled off the bed, bouncing off the floor for a second. "No, but I can finish it later!" I said.

"Look at you, mister!" he teased, and handed me my coat. "What do you have on under those?"

"PJ pants, one long sleeve, one thin sweater, and this," I said pinching the pants and sweater that covered all these layers.

He curled his lips in an upside-down smile, and then turned to the window. The light coming through the slats of the window blinds was turning burnt yellow, if not orange. The sun would soon set.

"That should do," he said. "Where is your scarf?"

"It's in my backpack."

He pulled my scarf from the backpack's front pocket and left the room. I heard him telling Mãe that he was taking me out while I struggled to get my shoes on over the wool socks our mother had also made.

"We'll be back for supper," he told her as I met them in the hallway. She had her hands wrapped up in a dishcloth.

"It's too cold today, honey. Are you sure you don't want to wait until tomorrow? It's supposed to warm up." She tilted her

39

head to the side as she took note of what we were wearing.

"Nah, we're tough." He smiled and looked at me. "Aren't we, *mano?*"

I nodded and he gave Mãe a loud kiss on her cheek.

"You two take care," she said. "I'll have some noodle soup ready for when you get back."

I kept my hands tucked into my armpits as we waited for a bus. The sun was making its way down, and a two-story home stood in the way of its warmth. Pablo watched, while people paced across the streets, rushing to get indoors and their fire working, racing against the sun itself. Every once in a while a sudden wind would blow, as if made up of little blades, cutting through your nostrils, and I would tuck my nose against my coat's shoulder pad.

The bus smelled of naphthalene and cigarettes and bad breath. Pablo wrinkled his nose and winked at me as we slowly made our way through its crowded corridor. We took the two window seats available on the right aisle, one in front of the other. Pablo took the one in front, and I just sat in the back. It was my first time riding a bus, and I remember thinking it looked a lot more fun from the outside than it actually was. There were quite a few empty seats, but for some reason a lot of people chose to not sit down. Maybe they were tired of sitting after a day's work, or maybe they were in for just one or two stops. I looked around at the passengers standing, some held on to the poles to keep themselves steady, while others, the taller ones, stretched their arms up to hold on to bars that ran along the entire ceiling. All of them seemed absent somehow. They didn't watch the road, or the other passengers. They were just there, their minds somewhere else.

The man sitting next to me was probably about thirty or forty years old, wearing mustard corduroy pants, a black jacket with a mismatched set of knitted gloves, scarf and a bonnet. He nodded at me as I went by him to take a seat, but something in the way he nodded made me think he didn't see me at all. Something about him wasn't really in that bus. I watched him for a moment, wondering what it would take to get his attention. His gloved hands rested on top of his brown leather suitcase, which he kept on his lap. His eyes gazed at the road ahead. As if he were a prop, and the sole purpose of his existence was to just be there, a blank figure to spark my curiosity.

I looked at Pablo. He was paying attention to the road, watching everything closely, as if afraid to miss our stop. I poked his shoulder with my finger.

"Where are we going?" I asked.

He struggled to look over his scarf "You'll see." He smiled, and went back to watch the city go by.

The windows were fogged with humidity and all the passengers' heat, so I used my elbow to clear an open view to the street. I knew I was about to learn something and I trusted that it would be something great. Pablo was with me that afternoon. I couldn't think of the last time he had taken me on an adventure, and I was bouncing in my seat.

We stopped at a traffic light in front of the City Hall, and right across the street was a wall with the words "THEY CAN'T SHUT US UP!" spray-painted in large, black graffiti. The message took up about ten meters worth of that wall. Its letters were sharp and slanted to the right, and I thought that whoever wrote them must have been left-handed just like me. Pablo stared at it as we waited for the green light, and something changed in his eyes; all of a sudden he had a more somber look on his face, more jaded. I feared he would change his mind about this trip after all and take me back to the house. But traffic moved along, and our surroundings eventually changed. We were driving by Parque Marinha, a new, gigantic public park. Its trees closest to the street looked fairly young as if they had been planted not long ago. But some vaster and richer trees stood farther out, closer to Rio Guaíba. Their crowns were gleaming as the sun made its way down behind them. It was beautiful. Pablo just glanced at them absentmindedly.

Close to the very end of the park there were about ten officers on horses, baton in hand, approaching a group of men that sat by its fountain. By the time the bus drove by them, everybody had their hands above their heads, as these officers created a sort of a circle around them.

"This is going to be a stadium," said Pablo, pointing at a construction site right by Rio Guaiba. "Inter is gonna play here someday."

"Cool."

The place was a huge artificial bank they'd built into the lake, where they were dumping sand as we passed. Trucks were already driving over what had always been just water. A city expanding its limits. I had never seen a stadium in real life, but I hoped that Pablo and I would get to watch a game there someday. He used to spend most of his free time playing soccer back home, whenever he didn't feel like hanging out in the tool shed, anyway. Every once in a while he'd teach me a few moves; but he always said one doesn't learn to play soccer through lessons, one learns by playing, and he mostly just showed off and beat me in every game.

"That's us here," said Pablo as he got up to pull on the cable that rang a bell.

I followed and almost fell over him as the bus came to a complete stop. We got out at a busy street corner. It must have been a little after 5pm and the sun felt good on my cheeks. Pablo pointed to one of the larger rocks by the lake, across the street from where we were. We waited for traffic to slow down, and ran to the other side – Pablo's hand on my elbow until we reached the sidewalk.

"Is that one good?" he asked, pointing at the large rock to the far left. Clearly placed on the sidewalk to serve as a bench, it sat underneath an enormous jacaranda tree, which had been stripped of most of its leaves with the coming spring. Although slanted, its surface looked polished and smooth from where we stood.

"I don't know." I pondered. "Is it?"

"Yeah, it's great!" He smiled and we both took a seat. We weren't the only ones there. There must have been about ten or fifteen people sitting, contemplating, smoking cigarettes and drinking *chimarrão*. Some were in groups while others sat by themselves. But even the ones that were talking didn't really look at each other. They just stared at the lake and the sun as conversations went back and forth. Pablo didn't look at me either, and I figured something was about to happen; I just wasn't sure what. I breathed on my fingers to fight the cold, and Pablo turned to me.

"Put your gloves on, man. It's cold."

"I think I left them in my backpack," I said.

"Here, take one of mine, then." He took one glove off and handed it to me. "Keep your good one warm. You never know when you might need to use it."

"Thank you." I put it on my left, and hid my right hand in between my legs like Pablo. He was watching the lake again. The street behind us was busy with rush hour traffic but its noise didn't seem to distract anyone but me.

"How are you doing, *mano*?"

"I'm good." I watched his profile. The sun made his face acquire a peachy shade, and Pablo suddenly looked healthier.

"Good. The sun is about to set," he announced.

"Is that why we're here?"

"Yes." He laughed, his breath cottony on the air. "People say this is the most beautiful sunset in the world. The longest, too." He nodded to add conviction.

"Oh," I'd seen the sun set a bunch of times, but never really watched it. "This is neat, Pablo," I said. "This is really nice."

"Like the old times, huh?" He looked at me. "You and me."

I nodded again. The lake lay still, smooth, mirroring the approaching sun, and glistening to create a beautiful dance of colors. People paid close attention to it, hoping to notice every shift, every nuance, everything that changed and everything that stayed the same as the sun slowly bowed for them. It was getting cold, but the air somehow seemed warmer. The orange, and pink, and purple, and white sparkles from the water, the scattered birds gliding across the sky reminded me of home, even though we didn't get sunsets like this back in Minas do Leão. Maybe it was just the fact that I was outside again. Or maybe it was because I was with Pablo.

At one point, I looked at him and noticed that he wasn't smiling anymore. He wasn't squinting at the direct light and all the colors like most of us either. Instead, he was frowning, not at the sun, but at whatever was going through his mind.

"Why do you think it's called Rio Guaíba if it's a lake?" I asked.

"No idea," he answered. "Maybe they just thought it was a river." He curled his lips.

I tried to warm my nose up by breathing into my cupped hand.

"Do you think they're right?" I asked.

"Right about what?"

"Do you think that's true, about the sunset?" I used my chin to point at the sun. "Is it really the most beautiful?"

"Oh." He paused. "Nah. I don't know. It's hard to tell, but I guess we're stuck with it, aren't we?" He elbowed me.

"I think it's neat."

"Yes. This is pretty neat." He put his arm around my shoulder. "Are you cold?"

I shook my head. "Nope."

People stuck around after the sun had already set with the same look in their eyes, a mixture of attentiveness and contemplation. It almost seemed as though they searched for something way beyond the actual spectacle, some kind of healing. The orange turned red, the red turned purple, the purple turned blue, and all of a sudden the lake didn't glisten anymore.

A young man who was sitting by himself on the sidewalk

placed his *cuia* on the ground, got up, and started to clap. All of us followed his lead, and after a while people began to gather their belongings and leave. Pablo saw each group disperse, and I watched Pablo.

"I miss home," I said quietly.

"I know." He looked down at his feet. "I miss it, too. But I think it's good that we're here, you know? I think we're meant to be here." He then got up and handed me his other glove. "Here, put this on. I'm not cold. Do you want to get going?"

"Sure," I said as I put his other glove on. I didn't want to leave. I wished the sunset had lasted a lot longer. Forever.

For years I questioned Pablo's belief that we were meant to be there. For years I thought that going to Porto Alegre was the worst thing that could've happen to all of us. I don't anymore.

. . .

Our father kept searching for jobs. Good jobs, that is. He was a proud man after all. But he began to get a disability check for the damage the coal had done to his lungs after so many years spent inside the mine, which was ironic since he'd taken up smoking again. Although we weren't struggling, we felt the changes. And they were drastic. We went from living in the best house in a small town, my father holding the highest position in that town, to being middle class nobodies in a ruthless city.

He'd say he hoped to decline the government help, he'd refer to it as tainted money, but after a while I guess he just gave in. Tainted money was still money.

Pablo had been involved with student organizations for as long as I remembered. Back then these groups gathered to talk about what the military coup had meant to their families, whether it was the loss of a job at the mine, or a parent who started drinking, or something else entirely. They needed to vent. But as the censorship grew tougher, Pablo became more distant, and his life more of a mystery to all of us. It wasn't overnight. Pablo changed a little every day; his hair was down to his shoulders, and was seldom washed. He tried to grow a beard, but it was too sparse, and it made him look more like the boy he was desperately trying to prove he no longer was.

For a while, our father would go to campus to search for Pablo whenever it was getting late, or whenever he just had a bad feeling. This emptiness right inside his stomach is what he'd say, which no food could suppress as much as our mother tried. But colleges became dangerous places. They were the stages where most movements were planned and managed; they were also infested with officers disguised as students. Since the government continued to monitor our father, he had to eventually keep his distance from campus, when rumors had spread that he was leading one of the revolutionary groups – his revenge for losing the mine.

What people usually find hard to believe is that while some lived in a constant state of fear there was still a choice to be made. And many, many people chose oblivion. Many believed the fight for survival was more dignified than the one for ideology. Many saw our rebels as hippies, or communists, or teenagers simply angry at the world, feeding off of these oppressors. I have many friends who still today are completely ignorant of what took place in our country during the Lead Years and those that followed. And for a while I was one of them. I did everything I could to ignore what was going on. I pretended that I didn't care, I'd kept on playing, watching and talking about soccer like everyone else, I focused on school, I tried to convince myself that Pablo was going through a phase, and that soon enough he'd find something else; a band, a new sport… something else to obsess over.

Pablo's class schedule at the university was all over the place, or so he told us, and most nights we wouldn't see him at all. I'd usually wait for him to come home at night. Maybe we all did. I'd be in my room with the window blinds partially open. Enough light would come in through the gaps to make out pretty much everything inside my room. We'd been living in that house for almost two years, but there was nothing familiar about it.

I would study this room that had become mine, but not. I'd listen to its sounds, to how the blinds vibrated when the *minuano* blew against them, to the way that outside noises penetrated its walls. I'd look at the light coming from underneath my bedroom door and study how each of the different lamps around the house would illuminate the room through the slit when switched on and off. I'd wonder who could've lived there, and whether or not they talked to each other. All these thoughts had never crossed my mind in the old house. I knew everything there was to know about it. I knew its sounds and its smells, the exact way the sunlight would hit its interior at any given moment, at any given season, which corners would collect the most black dust, which would first smell of mold after a week of torrential rain.

Sometimes, when I'd shut the blinds in this new room, its darkness reminded me of the galleries in the mine, and I could almost smell the intoxicating stench of sulfur again, the same smells Pablo and I played hide-and-seek in. I'd hold on to memories like this to stay awake. Once he finally got home, I would study the sounds on the other side of the wall. I would listen for the squeak of his wardrobe door opening then closing, I would hear the thump of his backpack against the wood floor, I listen to his steps across the hallway as he headed to the bathroom, then I'd wait for him to walk back again toward his room. I would pay attention to everything until there was nothing, and I'd imagine him asleep and wondered whether or not he had dreams similar to the ones I had; if whatever his fears were, if they continued to haunt him through the night.

. . .

On the last night my father went to campus after Pablo, he left our house at about 8pm. It wasn't that it was getting late, and it wasn't because Pablo had promised to be home early or anything. Pablo had gotten home at twelve the night before, and the lights in my parents' room had been out for at least two hours. My father just had a bad feeling that evening and couldn't wait any longer. Something about the way the clouds had opened themselves up to reveal the new moon and vanished just like that, or something about the pitch in the mosquitoes' buzz was just ominous, and my father couldn't contain himself.

He parked on a residential street across from campus. Families gathered around dinner tables, their silverware clinking against their colorful plates, their radios humming in the background. And he felt jealous of their mundane existence.

Campus wasn't as crowded as he'd seen it in the past, but plenty of students still walked around as if they had somewhere to go, while others sat against whatever they could find, smoking their cigarettes and sipping their *chimarrão*. My father headed for the Math building across from the broken water fountain with little expectation of finding Pablo where he actually belonged. The high ceilings and the marble floor of the building hallway echoed about four times over each time the sole of his shoes conquered more territory. He had seen Pablo there once, and ducked under the stairways to hide from his own son. On another time, he saw my brother sitting on a desk, talking about something he couldn't make out, while three other guys and one girl listened to Pablo in this otherwise empty classroom.

On that night though, it wasn't what he saw or heard that bothered him. Rather, it was what he felt. It was as if there was a presence of sorts watching him, following his every step. He wiped the sweat from his brow before looking back. But he couldn't see anything. He was alone in that hallway, and it seemed like a trap.

As uneasy as he felt, my father kept on walking, each step softer than the previous one, and after a while all he heard was his own breathing. The classroom where he had once found Pablo was empty except for one janitor who wiped the chalkboard with a wet rag. The janitor stopped and looked at my father as if wondering if he was lost. My father nodded but was ignored by the man, and kept on walking towards the library where he found dozens of people hiding behind their research, several of whom interrupted their reading to watch him wander through the hall. One man, who looked to be just a little younger than my father, too old to be a student, maybe a professor, he thought, got up and walked toward another older man. They both watched my father as they exchanged some hushed comments with one another. He had no doubt they were talking about him.

He picked up the first book he laid his hands on without even glancing at it, and pretended to look for a place to sit, while he scanned the building for Pablo, aware that the two men were still watching him. *I'm too old for this*, he thought. He put the book back on the mahogany bookcase, straightened his shirt and motioned toward the exit door as if he had suddenly realized he was needed somewhere. The two men dropped the books they were also pretending to look at, and left the library after my father.

As he stood outside, he considered the idea of trying the cafeteria to see if Pablo might be there. It was getting late, and there was no one in sight. Standing there alone, knowing that he was being watched, he thought about the mine, about the gravel underneath his boots, the familiar jokes his friends would tell. He thought about the way that the black powder turned into ink as he washed his hands after a day's work, the way it stained the basin. He rubbed the tip of his fingers against his thumb. His hands weren't as rough and calloused as they used to be. My father was growing soft and weak. What more could he do with his life? The mine was all he knew. A breeze suddenly picked up and swooshed against the back of his shirt, startling him. He knew nothing of his new life, except that it wasn't the one he had chosen. But it was.

He lit up a cigarette and headed back to his car.

After that night, my father settled for waiting for Pablo by our living room window, while he slowly sipped his *chimarrão*, eventually going through the entire thermos. He'd pull one of the kitchen chairs up to our front window and open up wide the flower printed curtains. My mother would carefully bring him the *cuia* and a thermos, place them on the windowsill, with the thermos still open for the water to cool down just enough for the first helping. Pai wouldn't take the couch, or one of the more comfortable chairs. Not once. He was afraid to fall asleep.

FIVE

WE SANG THE national anthem every Monday morning when we got to school, and every Friday at noon before we left. During the winter months, the early morning ceremony would be dreadful. Our minds barely awaken, our bodies struggling to keep warm as we breathed in frosty wet fog. But as the weather warmed, Fridays would be the worse; we'd be starving by noon, under the melting humidity, and everything seemed to drag on for hours before they released us.

Each grade would line up facing the large Brazilian flag on its mast, flowing in a subtle breeze, or hanging lazily still, but always, its seemed, bright and proud. We would stand still, both feet together, measuring our distance from each other with our outstretched right arm, our fingertips on the right shoulder of whoever was ahead of us. Our Moral and Civics Ed professor would face us to make sure everybody was in proper position. He too had something to prove. He would then bow discreetly, which meant it was time to cross our right arm, and place our hand over our heart, as the strident horns intro would soon begin and take us to our not-so beloved anthem.

They expected us to sing loudly while staring at that flag. Pedro always stood behind me, and would sometimes change the lyrics, make it into something funny and those of us around him would struggle to maintain a straight face. Anything he sang that wasn't the right words was funny. Anything. What was funny was how nervous we were for wanting to laugh. Every once in a while, officers would watch us perform. They usually came in pairs, and they would walk along the lines we had created, listening to our voices, making sure no one was lip-syncing. They would look at you sometimes, a stern glare in their eyes, and raise their hand, palm facing the sky, and motion that hand upward twice, to let us know we weren't doing a good enough of a job. 'Sing louder,' is what that hand was saying. A few times they would ridicule someone, tell them that the way they sang out of tune was a disgrace to the nation, that they should practice at home, and that if they couldn't get any better, that maybe they shouldn't sing at all, because they were spoiling it. I'd seen this happen at least twice. We were in sixth grade.

We had gotten used to having officers – or spies, as the boys called them – standing around our school every once in a while, or observing our lectures from the back of the room. Usually about two or three of them would circle through every classroom throughout the entire morning, and use recess and PE time to go through notebooks, and make sure we weren't deviating from the program.

On one of those mornings, I was playing soccer at recess, when Pedro whispered my name, as if attempting to pull some kind of trick, except we were playing for opposite teams that morning.

"They are calling your name," he said quietly, his teeth clenched, his lips barely moving, and his eyes as big and round as two oversized *jabuticabas*.

"Really?" I frowned, and immediately thought of Pablo.

"Just don't say anything, they won't know you're you," Pedro offered. But I was worried they had something important to say about Pablo. I walked up to them.

"Did you call Luca Fonte?"

"Is that you, kid?" The guard stepped on a cigarette butt and immediately lit another, cocking his head, like every detective you see in movies.

"I am Luca Fonte," I said.

"Well, you come with me then. There's something we need to ask you."

Inside the classroom, another guard waited for me, puffing smoke. He was standing by my desk, staring at my notebook, as if hypnotized by it.

"Have a seat, boy." He didn't look at my face. I sat down and saw the message I had written over and over on the very last page of my notebook. "Can you tell me what the hell is this?" he asked.

I could feel my entire spine buckle, as if I was about to disintegrate in front of these men. I shook my head. Whatever happened, whatever they had in mind for me, I couldn't tell them the truth about those words.

"So you write things that you don't know what they are."

I nodded.

"Do you speak?"

"It's just something I saw once, on my way to school. That's all." I didn't dare to look at him. "It was a long time ago," I said.

I thought of the meaning of this message I was getting in trouble for writing, "They can't shut us up!" I thought about how quiet his presence had made me. And a sob came from deep inside my chest. Not only because of my predicament at that very moment, but because of Pablo's, and anybody else with similar illusions.

"Let me get this straight. you see a random message on your way to school, you get here, you don't pay attention to your class. Instead you spend, what, fifteen, twenty minutes rewriting it over and over, even though it means absolutely shit to you?!"

I cringed at the word 'shit' exactly like the child he saw in front of him, and I cried like one. I wanted to go back. To unwrite it. To go all the way back in years, where I still was climbing avocado trees with Clara, or zipping through the mine's tunnels.

"Boy, you're lucky you are an idiot," said the mustached man with a beer belly as he flipped his cigarette butt out the window. "Now get the hell outta here. But I'll be watching you, Luca Fonte."

...

My mother always said that ever since we were little, that Pablo and I would both talk in our sleep. She actually said we'd yell to

53

each other. I'd be in my room, Pablo in his. Sometimes she'd say one or both of us would sit up and carry a conversation on as if the other was just across an imaginary table. She'd say that it clearly sounded like a dialogue, that she recognized something of a question and answer pattern to our exchanges. Sometimes it sounded like an argument, a heated discussion, except we both spoke in a different dialect, something she couldn't understand nor recognize. So it could just be like German, she'd say, where even *I love you* can sound like an insult to the untrained ear. But she insisted that we clearly understood one another. In the morning Mãe would try to reenact our late night's exchange, and Pablo and I would laugh out loud at the way she spoke. Neither one of us remembering anything, neither one of us intrigued.

. . .

His name was Edson Luís de Lima e Souto; and while some people say he had no business being at Restaurante Calabouço on the evening of March 28, 1968, others guarantee it was his mission in life to represent a generation. A courageous, skinny boy of only eighteen, he found himself protesting against the restaurant's high prices and the decrease in quality of the food they served. Edson Luís was accompanied by a legion of students, the restaurant's clientele, when armed soldiers arrived with the intention of dispersing the crowd. While some people left, fearing the situation could escalate to dangerous proportions, others took refuge inside the restaurant they were protesting against. Edson Luís among them.

It didn't take long for the army to start threatening with shots, tear gas grenades, and for the crowd to respond with rocks, sticks, chairs, and whatever they could get their hands on. It was a warm evening, and they quickly began to sweat underneath their t-shirts and shorts as they scrambled against one another just because they couldn't stay still. They were unprepared and vulnerable. Most of all, they were astonished by the army's extreme reaction, which until that night was unheard of. Edson Luís, who hadn't been in Rio de Janeiro long enough to know his way around that big city, couldn't even understand how he had gotten himself into that situation, and how the situation dramatically changed in a matter of seconds.

The people around him yelled orders at each other, some of which were to quit the yelling. They yelled at the army, saying how all of it had to be a misunderstanding, they argued with one another until each of them noticed the first person around them being injured by the army's attack. And then they yelled at God.

The violent but still somewhat naïve exchange didn't last very long until the army decided to invade the restaurant where Edson Luís took shelter with his peers. By then one of his flip-flops had already ripped after being stepped on by someone else, and the other was lost. The police, the army, or the government, whatever name they wished to use under the circumstance, advanced quickly, yelling obscenities at these young men, as if they were criminals. Most of which Edson Luís wouldn't dare repeat. Later, they would declare that they had reason to believe the students were about to invade the United States Embassy. That would be the first of many times they would justify themselves in a similar fashion. The threat those students posed on that night led to a bloody raid. During the raid, one of the commanders took aim at our barefooted boy with a point-blank shot into his eighteen-year-old chest. Edson Luís died instantly.

Fearing that the army could hide the boy's body and deny what had just taken place, students stood by him and did not allow them to take him to the forensic institute. Instead, the crowd organized themselves, and marched to the Legislative Assembly of Rio de Janeiro with a blood-stained Brazilian flag covering Edson Luís' body. The crowd, which gradually multiplied, walked very slowly. Not because they wished to linger, but because they feared any sudden movement could spark yet another confrontation. The boy was later buried to the sound of the national anthem sung a capella by the crowd present at the impromptu ceremony.

Edson Luís was one of the very first students ever killed by our military dictatorship and between his funeral and the seventh day mass we would witness the first organized protests against the coup, this time throughout the entire country. The photo of his dead body covered by our tainted flag would make its way to most newspapers across the nation, since censorship hadn't yet been established. The quality of most pictures I saw was low, the print too dark, and you could hardly see Edson Luís' face. But one thing was very clear. And that was the look of tremendous fear in the eyes of those who dared to carry his body, those who dared to look after this boy. These young men were the very first to stand up against this new enemy they knew nothing about.

On the very next day, Cinelândia changed all the titles of movies being shown at its premises. The glamorous theater in downtown Rio de Janeiro closed its doors, refusing to indulge in any kind of entertainment while the country should be grieving. The new movie titles they advertised were "The Night of the Generals. Point Blank," "Heart of Grief," "Do Bullets Kill Hunger?" and what would later become the slogan of many organized movements, "They killed a student. What if it had been your son?"

. . .

We barely saw Pablo in the week following Edson Luís' death. My father read and reread every article regarding the boy, as if he could've missed some information the first time around. It was customary for him to collect old newspapers in a basket by the fireplace to help start the fire when winter came, but this time the pages were all over our living room. The coffee table was buried underneath mismatched sections of the paper he didn't see of value: the sports section, classifieds…

On the couches he placed the stories he wished to save.

These were everything he had come across regarding what had happened in that restaurant and what followed. They included op-eds, subsequent protests, some of Edson Luís' family members coming forward to express their astonishment and to talk about the kind of boy he was.

My mother seemed more obsessed with tending to the house. That week she climbed onto a chair and cleaned every single spider web in every upper corner of every room. She also took every piece of lining out of the kitchen cabinets and sponged them to perfection, then put them all back up again, polishing every piece of silver we still had left before placing them back where they belonged. She also reorganized every closet, she polished her shoes, and she took out the crochet linings of each dishcloth and crocheted everything back again. The entire house, except for the living room, was sparkling clean.

Tia Mercedes called one afternoon, and my mother took a deep breath when I handed her the phone receiver. From my bedroom I could hear her

"And how is Junior doing?" she asked. Nothing about the pitch in her voice exposed how quiet she had been all week.

"Oh, we're great! Pablo just *loves* college. I mean, he's a great student, thank God, but he sure is having fun!" It actually hurt my ears to listen to her, but I couldn't bring myself to shut the door.

"Well, dear, I have to go to church now so I can get back in time to fix supper." She said, "*Ah, sim*! Well, you know. Turns out the prayers relax me." She sounded more like herself then.

"Give little Junior a kiss for me, will you? I hope to meet him soon!"

"*Beijo. Tchau.*"

I shut my bedroom door when she was finished. But by the time I sat back on the floor to do my homework, my mother opened the door again to ask if I needed anything. "No," I said. I couldn't look at her.

I didn't understand why we couldn't talk about what was

going on, until one day I walked into the kitchen and saw my father taping his newspaper clippings to the fridge. He had carefully taken out the magnets that Mãe collected and made sure to bring to Porto Alegre, and one by one, he pasted what *he* had collected over the course of that week.

A picture of Edson Luís' body covered by the bloody flag was taped at eye level. Right below was another shot of that same scene, except panned out, and you could see the crowd that had gathered around him. To the right a picture of some armed soldiers, with a caption below asking "How far will they go?" And right below this one, a photo of what was left of that restaurant. Broken windows, half of a table sticking out of one. The bar completely destroyed and what used to be a bomboniere laid sideways, shattered – lollipops, *rapaduras*, Ping-Pong gum, and *paçocas* spread across the floor, stepped on, crushed. The restaurant's owner posed for the photographer right in front of what used to be the establishment's main entrance. He was of medium height, wearing soccer shorts, a light tee shirt and *havaianas*. His head was balding, and his face was the face of hopelessness.

As my father arranged everything, my mother stood by the sink, crying over chopped onions. Nobody talked. When she needed something from the fridge, she would just stand there in silence, behind my father, hoping he would somehow sense her presence and excuse himself to allow her to do her job. He wouldn't try to exchange small talk or apologize for any inconvenience his presence could be causing her. I sat in the living room and watched through the hallway how the two circled around each other. There was something maniacal in the way my father worked. He was focused but also oblivious to anything else. While the onions sizzled on the frying pan my mother quickly wiped the counter, stopping herself before getting too close to him.

At one point, the doorbell rang and Mãe rushed out of the kitchen, patting her hands against her apron. She glanced at the mess my father had made in the living room and shook her head as if to rid herself of it. It was Rita. She'd hardly come over. Her family had moved to Porto Alegre at about the same time we did. Rita and Pablo were still together. But we didn't see her as much as we used to back home, and I figured it was because we didn't see Pablo as much anymore.

"Hi Rose! Is Pablo around?"

I rushed to the door. Rita had changed a lot. She actually looked like she belonged to the city, with her faded jeans, her flip-flops, and her long braids.

"Ah, *oi* Luca! Come here and give me a hug!" Her smile remained the same. "I haven't seen you in such a long time. How is school?"

"Good. How are you?"

"Well, you know, hanging in there." She glanced at Mãe.

It never once crossed my mind to tell my parents what had happened to me at school. I thought about telling Pablo they had questioned me. I thought about telling him all that I knew, and asking him about all the things I didn't yet know. But I just never did. Watching Rita standing at our front door, I wanted to tell her. I wanted her to know that even though they made me cry, even though I had almost peed myself, I didn't give in.

"Rita, *querida*, Pablo isn't home. But would you like to come in and wait for him?"

Rita's smile was gone. She looked at her flip-flops, then slid both of her hands down her braids.

"Do you know what time he'll be back?" Her voice had changed too.

"No. We just never know with Pablo anymore. His classes. Just all over the place."

"*Sim.* I know." Her voice was bordering on despair. "Well, just tell him I stopped by."

"I will, dear. And you take care, okay?"

"Yeah," I added.

Both my mother and I hugged Rita before she left. My

father didn't make it out of the kitchen. He just kept on working.

"Luca, are you alright?" my mother asked as I headed back to my room.

I nodded.

. . .

When Pablo finally arrived we all sat around the kitchen table and ate Mãe's *carreteiro* in silence. Every once in while Pablo would steal glances at our father's work on the fridge. Pai rushed through his plate while Pablo took his time almost as if trying to postpone whatever would come after dinner.

"This is delicious, Mãe," he said.

I agreed and Mãe smiled then looked at the way our father was eating, but didn't say anything. Pai scraped his plate then immediately got up and placed it in the sink. He turned around and looked at us for not more than a second, then said, "Rose, Luca, I need to talk to Pablo about something. Can you excuse us, please?"

Pablo rolled his eyes. I still had food in my mouth.

My mother and I got up, leaving our plates as they were. I left the kitchen and headed to my room. My mother was already in the hallway, and when she turned to enter her room, I noticed the rosary dripping off of her right hand. It was the first time I had seen her with it around the house.

When their argument became too loud, my mother came over to my room to check on me. I was sitting on my bed, watching the door, trying to hear and process everything they were saying, and trying to ignore them at the same time. She just looked at me and shut the door again.

. . .

It is the middle of the night and everybody is asleep. I wake up drenched in sweat and go to the kitchen for a glass of iced water. The light post right out front shines through the window, hitting the fridge, where my father's clippings still remain. I stand there reading his work. The night-light seems to hide the pictures' imperfections. I see real people around that boy's body. I see tears in their eyes. I sense the fear in their breaths.

I search for the one picture I had seen was a close-up. I want to see Édson Luis' face in this light. I want to see what an accidental rebel looks like. I want to know if there is fear beyond death like they say there is peace. But instead of Édson Luis, I see Pablo's skinny body covered by the bloody flag, his eyes shut, his lips slightly parted. I look at all the other pictures and they are all of my brother.

Pablo dead underneath the flag.

Pablo crouching right by his own lifeless body.

Pablo looking straight into the reporter's camera.

Pablo carrying a banner denouncing the atrocity.

Pablo posing in front of a broken restaurant.

Pablo singing at the burial…

I leave the kitchen disoriented trying to find my way to his bedroom. But the door is locked, and it won't even wiggle as I push and pull it. It feels like it's been glued to its frame. I look at its frame, studying it in the dark, searching for what could have jammed it that way. I switch the light on and am sick to my stomach when I find right above it:

Pablo Fonte
1949-1968
Your memory will live on
in those who remain

SIX

THE FOUR OF US sat around the kitchen table again early the next morning for breakfast. Outside the day was white, yet Pai's clippings still taped to our fridge seemed as though they cast a shadow over us. He flipped through his newspaper, much like he had done all week, slowing down at a sports op-ed, the day's featured crime, a catastrophic accident at BR-116 and finally the cover article, an interview with Edson Luis' father.

Mãe didn't touch her scrambled eggs. She'd sip her coffee every once in a while, play with the slice of bread on her plate, pull tiny little crumbs, and place them on her lips or let them fall on the table. Twice I saw her look at our father then search something else in the kitchen to inspect. A cracked tile, a drawer that wouldn't shut all the way.

Pablo quickly devoured everything that was on his plate and downed his chocolate milk in one gulp.

"Mãe, I have a project I need to research at lunch time. Don't wait for me, okay?" Pablo said as he grabbed two bananas off the kitchen counter.

"Okay, *filho*. Why don't I make you a sandwich then?"

"No need." He waved the two bananas at her.

"Alright. You take care," she said as he leaned to kiss her forehead. "*Te amo, meu filho.*"

. . .

"Luca, we're out of beans. I'll be right back," Mãe said before closing the door behind her.

Three hours later, she came back with beans and a statue of Nossa Senhora Aparecida, which she placed over a crochet napkin, on the fireplace mantel. Although far from being an atheist, our mother was never one to go to church every week, or pray every day. She believed in the power of faith, of any kind. She embraced all religions and exercised none, except for special occasions or requests. But soon after we moved to Porto Alegre, Mãe changed the way she felt about faith. She figured that by accepting everything, she was bound to be neglected by all of them.

While the pressure pot whistled, Mãe rearranged all the little trinkets we already had on the mantel to make sure the statue was properly featured; her pink rosary carefully draped over Nossa Senhora's shoulders. She placed the telephone Pai had purchased at the very corner, wiping the dust from underneath it. How methodical both of them could be on the verge of fear. It seemed so strange to watch her now go through this dance, after what our father had done with the clippings. She was calm though. Thorough. She'd test what the little silver picture frame looked like to the left of the Saint. She'd take a few steps back, tilt her head, stare at it for a second, then move it a few inches closer. Her own mother's smile in the picture despite her fragile figure after battling cancer for years was a symbol of the strength women carried in the family, a reminder to my mother. She grabbed a saucer from the kitchen cabinet and placed it between her mother's photo and the Saint, with a lit candle on it.

She stepped back again, studied her little altar, then headed to her bedroom. When she came back she had two 3x4 photos, one of Pablo and one of me, and she leaned them on both sides of her mother's picture frame. She then headed back to the kitchen, from where she brought a small glass vase with daisies.

Mãe studied it for about a minute.

"What do you think, Luca? Does it look desperate?" she asked.

She knew I was watching her from my room. "It's beautiful, Mãe." I said, and she smiled.

My mother grabbed a lambskin rug from her bedroom and laid it by the fireplace, where she knelt to whisper her prayers. The candle flickered as a cool breeze came in from the chimney, and Mãe looked up, stretching her neck as if to welcome this sudden relief.

The smell of beans was gradually taking over our home as the pressure pot whistled louder still. But her eyes were shut. She was alone.

. . .

Time mystifies life. The more we distance ourselves from an event, the more power it attains.

It was December 1968. An old, traditional clock hung on the wall behind President Costa e Silva marking 6pm. He sat at the very end of a big oval table, next to Vice-President Pedro Aleixo. Ministers, secretaries, and other top officials joined them. Name tags had been placed in front of each man along with a tall glass of iced water, while two recorders sat at the center of the lustrous mahogany table. It was a dark room lit by a chandelier made up of burnt yellow bulbs. Men smoked cigarettes and celebratory cigars even before the meeting had started. Through the smoke, one could see a large Brazilian flag hanging on a slanted post coming out of the opposite wall where the President sat. The medals and pins on the men's uniforms seemed to shine more through that artificial fog and warm lights. President Costa e Silva watched while everybody settled in their seats with excitement. Mr. Aleixo, on the other hand, focused on the sweat forming around his glass of water.

A crowd of protesters outraged by the secrecy of this meeting had gathered outside the building. Most of them weren't part of any movement against the dictatorship, but rather government employees who had spent the day inside that same building now guarded by soldiers forming a human chain.

To the politicians inside, they chanted indistinct accusations, occasionally followed by orders, also indistinct, through a megaphone. The men present at that meeting smiled as if amused by the childish fussiness that penetrated their walls.

"Good evening, Gentlemen," the President began. "As we

all know, our revolution is in jeopardy. Our democracy is at risk as long as we continue to allow such protests against the Union." He took a sip of water. "Difficult times call for difficult decisions."

Vice-President Aleixo shifted in his seat, realizing how wrong that after-hour meeting was. A formality, really, to document what had already been decided in private conversations. He wondered if there was even a point in repeating himself. Argue for the sake of argument, or argue for the sake of maintaining a clean conscience. Sirens blasted outside as the protest intensified.

"This is exactly what I'm talking about," President Costa e Silva jumped in as if on a cue, holding his finger up, silencing all men, and all they heard was the protest and the rolling of the tape inside both recorders. "We are losing control of the situation." He paused to look at each of his men, all of whom met him with reassuring gazes. All except for Mr. Aleixo, who reached for his water instead. Annoyed, the President continued on, "I would like to hear your thoughts on the Institutional Act – Number 5, being proposed at this time."

Mr. Aleixo cleared his throat. His heart throbbed with rage, disgust and fear above anything else. It was risky to pose an argument against the most powerful men in the country. It was almost suicidal to do such a thing when he knew he was alone in that fight. Several politicians had already been arrested.

"With all due respect, Mr. President, although I agree that this time calls for some kind of reaction, we can't ignore that the amendment being proposed today is going completely against the principles of democracy, Sir." His eyelids twitched.

"This is a time for actions and not for principles, Mr. Vice-President," argued Minister Passarinho. His thick glasses couldn't disguise his determination. "In fact, the situation has escalated in such way, I actually think this amendment is not strict enough." President Costa e Silva smiled proudly at Mr. Passarinho's remarks.

Outside, soldiers laughed at their countrymen, at how

ridiculously desperate they seemed.

"I work here!" one man yelled with his hands tied behind his back. A soldier used his own tie to shut his mouth. Sweat collected on his forehead as he thought about how quickly he could be sent to one of the basements he had heard about, and how fast one can switch sides in a system like ours. He thought of his wife and son waiting at home.

"This is insane!" another man cried as he saw his coworker being humiliated by some twenty-year-olds.

"They can't do this. It's against the constitution!"

"They *are* the constitution!"

Outside, the crowd became larger and louder. Inside, the officials remained monotone. Only Mr. Aleixo couldn't contain himself. "Gentlemen, we should consider the radical nature of our actions."

But the President was clearly bored already. "Why don't we stop wasting everybody's time and just take a vote?"

...

While this meeting was taking place I was at home, and so was Pablo.

He paced around his room as if he were packing to go somewhere. Every once in a while I could hear his hushed phone conversations with four or five different people. He spoke in codes, it seemed. A collection of monosyllabic words, which I understood as something I shouldn't understand.

"*Aparelho?*" I was pretty sure that's what he said.

"No. Two," he said.

"Wall… Can't… Out…" I heard at one point.

I went up to his room and stood by the door, watching as Pablo bent his entire body over the open window. I could see flames and smoke lighting up the night sky right outside, and since the trashcan in his room was missing, I figured he was responsible for the flames I was looking at. He held a handful of papers in his hand when he turned to look at me, which he immediately threw into this fire as a reflex.

"What's going on?" I asked.

He had no shirt on. His spine stuck out like that of a malnourished child.

Startled, he bumped his head on the windowpane; his hair sprinkled with specks of ash. He quickly shut the window. Fire through glass. He didn't look at me at first, but moved around the room skimming the messy floor. On his neck, he had on our mother's necklace. The pendant, São Jorge on his horse; a warrior. She must have given it to him.

"Just getting rid of some old school papers. Who wants to keep those, right?" He smiled and walked over to the pile waiting for incineration, picked it up, and hid the whole thing inside a drawer. Pablo would always smile and tuck his hair behind both ears when caught off guard or lying. It was almost like a tic.

He suddenly seemed immature to me, so naïve for thinking no one knew what he was up to, and for believing he would get something out of it. I hated his hope.

"Pablo, we're not dumb, you know?"

"What are you talking about?" His eyes scanned the entire bedroom one more time.

"Mãe is getting sick from worrying about you. Can't you see what you're doing to her? To us? You know she goes to church every day now?"

He grabbed his brown flannel shirt and while he was putting it on I could almost see a hint of his old self in his eyes. He sat on his bed, tapping on it two or three times to invite me to sit.

"Luca." He rested his right hand on my knee. "You have to promise me you will never talk about this to anyone." I nodded. "You don't understand, Luc. Things have changed. These people… They think they can…" I could feel the blood rushing through my head as I listened to his speech. "It's our *duty*…," he continued, his voice shaky. "We can't let this happen. Only *we* can stop this. And we will." He kept checking the time on his watch.

He noticed I was looking at Mãe's necklace, and he held on to São Jorge.

"Mãe gave it to me after that last argument with Pai. For protection, she said." He let out a somewhat sad smile.

"It sounds like you need it," I said. "Alright Pablo, I think I'm going to bed." I didn't look at him as I headed to my room.

"Luca," he called. I could hear the lump in his throat.

I turned to find him sitting on the bed. His eyes were welling up. Those were the eyes I knew, except for the sadness in them.

"I love you," he said.

"I love you too, Pa."

He wiped his tears with the sleeve of his flannel shirt – his favorite. I will spend the rest of my life wishing that I had shown him that the love I had for him was enough to make me cry too.

...

The next day, the streets were almost deserted, and the few people who crossed my path had an urgency to their pace that kept them from looking me in the eye. I hadn't seen Pablo at breakfast, and wondered if he could also be rushing by me, not noticing. A sun-fired fog, thick as a dream, covered the streets, making the usual dense and humid air feel heavy as a cloud. Fogged windows secluded life inside the homes along the way, and street dogs rested on the sidewalks, following my steps with their eyes while the tips of their tails gently tapped the warm concrete, as if saying "I'm here, if you feel like petting me."

I had never seen as many officers at school as I did on that day. Hanging around its front gate, talking to each other by the R.V. snack bar, watching while boys played soccer, walking through its corridors, peeking through classroom doors. Just about everywhere you looked.

Prof. Caetano, our Social Studies teacher, seemed very different that morning. He wore a tan suit with bell-bottoms, and his long hair was neatly swiped to the back with the help of a lot of gel. The first time I had ever seen him wear a suit, as he'd usually stick to the school's uniform and sneakers. But that morning he looked sharp. I liked Prof. Caetano. He always found a way to talk about the things everyone seemed to avoid. And he was creative about it too. Ever since the censorship got tougher, he adopted a few metaphors, nicknames for things he shouldn't be talking about, but which we all intuited.

"Hello, my children!" he began with what seemed like a forced cheerful tone. "Today is a very special day! Do you know why?"

"It's Friday!" said Pedro.

"Well, that too. But not just any Friday." He looked towards the door. "Today we wake up to everything that has been going on for far too long."

His voice was getting a little shaky, and he glanced at the door again. Pedro and I looked at each other for a second.

"Today we finally see our government for what it is: a dirty, disgusting dictatorship."

No codes. No metaphors. As clear and as plain as it could be. The words were heavy to hear, a burden unasked for, a mass of karma, fear, and responsibility. It was the very first time I felt as though the changes had reached *me*. Not my father, not my brother, but me.

"Listen to me. Listen carefully," he said. "*I voted* in 1960. *I voted.*"

He talked with a bitter nostalgia about the times when democracy was still in place. He took his time with his words, as if to allow each one inside that classroom enough of a chance to register their meaning.

"*I voted,*" he repeated one more time.

Two officers were peeking through the door, and Prof. Caetano looked at them, then at his polished shoes, and back to us again. "This whole thing won't go on forever. I promise. This isn't our country. This is not our Brasil."

The two officers yanked the door open and walked fast towards our teacher. One of them had a smile on his face like a kid who had been waiting for his turn on the ghost train at the city fair. The other officer had a look of rage and disgust. When close enough, he spit on our classroom floor, next to Prof. Caetano's shoes.

I recognized him from the time they had questioned me. He had watched the whole thing quietly on that day.

"I'm sorry you have to see this." Prof. Caetano said to us, and then turned to the man who was cuffing him. He was short and chubby, definitely younger than our teacher. "Actually, I'm glad you saw it. We won't give our country up that easily." He smiled.

As they were about done cuffing our teacher, his back turned to us, his face pressed against the chalkboard, Prof. Caetano fought his way off of their grasp, then turned to us again. "Down with the dictatorship!" He yelled. All veins bulging in his neck. It seemed loud enough for the entire school to hear.

The quiet officer slammed his baton hard against Prof. Caetano's ribcage. A few girls yelled in shock. Our teacher was left quietly gasping for air.

Juliana, the girl who always sat in the front row, hid her face on her desk. I could see the spasms her whole body fought through to keep her sobs to herself. Other kids placed their elbows on their desks and covered their eyes with their hands. I had seen "Down with the dictatorship" all over town, but the words had never carried as much meaning to me as they did coming out of Prof. Caetano's mouth that morning.

"Whatever makes you happy, punk!" the officer replied with a smirk. He turned to us. "And you better see what happens to idiots like this one!" He watched our teacher, who'd become quiet, struggling to regain control of his breathing.

They waited inside the classroom until recess, harassing Prof. Caetano, talking about the things most of us had never heard, about the different types of torture there were, the horrible food that most mutts would decline, the isolation, about how he would never see his family again. Every once in a while, they'd smack and punch our teacher, as if to remind him of what they were capable.

"Aren't you ashamed? Look at what you're putting your students through," said one of the officers, shaking his head from side to side.

Prof. Caetano didn't say anything. And with his baton, the officer hit the back of his knees, bringing our teacher to the floor instantly.

"When I ask, you respond. *Capiche*?" He stared at our teacher.

Pedro was pale, and I could hear people fighting through their tears, afraid to call attention to themselves. And Fernando, our classroom clown, who never missed an opportunity to make fun of anyone, had peed himself, urine dripping from the front of his chair and gradually darkening his pants. No one dared to say anything or even look at him. All you could hear was the officers' occasional laughter and the sound of my classmates sniffling, as tears fell on their desks.

At recess, they took our teacher down by the school bar. He was no longer resisting their commands, and still they knocked him down, and smacked him several times with more force each time. It was clear they were having fun.

It felt as if I had numbed myself while I focused on everybody else. None of us really knew what we were supposed to feel, or how we were supposed to behave in the presence of these men. And after it was all over, nobody talked about it. No one, not the principal, not the teacher who we had after recess, not the students either. No one mentioned what had taken place. As if there was nothing to explain.

When we were finally allowed to leave, there were at least twenty officers standing at the school's front gate, and many others slowly riding their horses, in circles, along my way home. People didn't talk to one another like they usually did after class. Everybody went about their own lives, avoiding eye contact with the guards and each other. We kept our distance from any soldiers, but we all watched, from the corner of our eyes, from the reflection of a window, from the safety of school buses. All of us saw those men enjoying the thrill of the power they held, the pleasure they felt by intimidating us all.

As I made my way towards our house, I noticed that the graffiti message "They can't shut us up!" had been covered with paint and a photo of Brasil's president wearing a military uniform covered in medals and pins and ribbons, all of which reminded me of Clara, and how beautiful she was. I wondered if she still collected pins, if she still thought about where each should go on her wardrobe. I wondered how she liked Caxias do Sul. Standing across that wall, I thought about removing the President's poster – that's what Pablo would have done – or maybe rewriting the original message over his face. But I wasn't like my brother.

Instead I just stood there, staring at that man. He looked as if he could be any man. As if he could be one of the miners who had walked away with my father. But there, on that wall, shutting up those words, with the golden embroidery on his lapel, and the polished pins and buttons, and the bushy eyebrows, and the lustrous forehead, I couldn't help but question my judgment. His eyes gazed to the side, as if looking above your shoulder, as if you were too small to be noticed, too insignificant. His forehead had a deep vertical line running through it, because he had too much to take care of, greater things on his mind, things beyond our understanding. Standing there watching him, as conscious as a fourteen-year-old kid could be of his own reality, of his own people, it seemed as though on that day everything was memorable.

But it would take me years to understand what it was really about. People talked about censorship, about freedom of speech. But the reality was far more frightening. On that day, the government had passed a new law behind closed doors revoking our constitution, one that would last for ten years and wipe out the main privileges democracy guaranteed. In one day, idealists, students, artists, and politicians who dared to criticize the state became criminals. Newspapers would print full black pages – their way of showing us the censorship had been there. Metaphors became the only tool a writer or a musician had to get his frustration across without disappearing. From then on, fathers, daughters, and many sons would vanish, leaving behind scattered clues for their families to delve into, or simply block from their memories in fear of losing each other. All we knew was that some were killed, some were tortured then killed, some were jailed, and the luckier few were sent into exile.

. . .

"We need a family meeting," Mãe told me as I dropped my backpack by the kitchen door.

The moment she realized how bleak the words had come out of her mouth, she shook her head as if to rid herself of that other person who she was gradually becoming. She gave me a kiss on the forehead, as she'd always done, except this time she cradled my head with both her soft, warm hands, and released a deep breath, like she'd been holding it since I left for school.

"*Filho*, do you want a snack?" She moved quickly and aimlessly around the kitchen, as if trying to remember where the pantry could possibly be. She stopped herself, and noticed my stare. She smiled. "I keep getting the kitchens mix up. Keep thinking we're still back home."

"This is home, Mãe."

"I know. Here," she said as she opened the bread basket inside the pantry. "I'll make you a ham sandwich."

"I'm not hungry yet. *Obrigado*," I said. "Mãe, where's everybody?" I took a seat at the linoleum kitchen table.

Mãe couldn't possibly know what had happened at school. This meeting couldn't be about that. I started to wonder if maybe they had gone to every school, if Pablo had endured a similar situation at his university. Then I thought about the things he had been doing, and his behavior the night before, and a knot began to form in my throat and my heart seemed to want to jump out of my mouth.

"How was school today, honey?" She clasped her hands and paced around the kitchen. Her slippers swept the immaculate tiles in short and stubborn sweeps, a sound that had always annoyed her and that she would do her best to prevent. She filled up a jar of water and started to bathe the flowerpots sitting by the tall windowsill.

"It's too damp today, I'm not even sure they're thirsty."

It was a very warm and humid spring that year, and as we moved through December there was no hope for relief coming any time soon. My mother would constantly pat dry the inside walls with bath towels to avoid mold, go through the entire house working from top to bottom, delicately drying each wall as if they were children, pruning after a long bath. But water would seep through the wall the moment she stopped. That would become yet another thing she could not avoid, however hard she tried.

I watched her go through the motions, as she always did. Her hand trembled as she struggled to maintain only a small stream of water coming out of that jar, and not drown her precious daisies. Specks of dust danced in a beam of light coming from our kitchen window, illuminating her chest, where her São Jorge necklace used to be.

"You never told me how your school was today," she said.

"It was okay, I guess. Prof. Caetano was taken by the guards," I said. She tilted her head. However mad I was at myself for telling her, it wasn't enough to make me stop. "It was quite a scene. They were everywhere. A bunch of them on horses, while…"

"Your father went to find Pablo," she interrupted. "His class should've been over at twelve but he hasn't shown up yet."

The image of Pablo looking at me the night before as I was

about to leave his room popped into my head.

"Did you hear him this morning? I didn't see him leave. He never wakes up that early," she continued, laying the jar upside down on the counter and caressing the petals of her daisies. "Oh! I'm sorry, dear!" she said after bruising one petal.

"Who? Pablo? Or Dad? Dad had breakfast with us, Mãe. Are you okay?"

She shook her head again.

"Would you like some tangerine juice? I squeezed some this morning. They were very sweet." She forced a smile while her eyes remained distant and her brows tensed. Grabbing an acrylic jar out of the refrigerator, she inched it closer to her face and smiled again, reminding me of something you'd see on a TV commercial. I nodded, and she headed for the kitchen counter. Her slippers sweeping against the floor, untamed. Halfway to the counter the jar suddenly slipped from her fingers, crashing on the white tiles, spilling over her slippers and shins.

"Shit," she said quietly, but it wasn't enough. *"Que merda! Merda, merda, merda!"*

"Wait, Mãe. Let me do it." I grabbed some cloths from underneath the kitchen sink and began to soak them. My mother knelt next to me, staring at the orange puddle, and started to cry almost as quietly as the girls in my class.

"He's fine, Mãe. He's probably studying at the library." I couldn't really look at her or else she would see that I hardly believed it myself, but I had to say something.

When I finished cleaning, I watched as she stared at the distance, until I noticed her eyes searching mine. I headed for the TV.

"Don't you turn the TV on!" she yelled.

"Okay, I'm sorry!"

"Oh, honey, I just have a really bad headache. I'll lie down when your father comes back. *Desculpa eu.*"

My mother and I waited in silence by the living room window just like my father had done many times since we had moved there.

There are times when it feels as though events rush through you, forcing themselves onto everything you know, pushing their new folds whether or not you are living through them. And there are times when it seems as though everything stops, and you almost question your own existence as you wait for something completely outside of your own body to determine who you are going to be for the rest of your life. As we waited, I looked at my own reflection in the window, feeling completely powerless over everything, and I wondered if such feelings leave us at one point, if adulthood came with certain commodities such as knowing who you are, and who you will be on the next day. I turned to face my mother, as she stared at the orangey wood floor, waxed the day before by her own tireless hands. Hands that hid behind her elbows as she rested her crossed arms over her soft stomach. Her hazel eyes were drowning in a kind of fear I may never understand. And suddenly I was absolutely sure that my mother was just as helpless as I was.

"Mãe, would you like some chimarrão?" I asked her, in an effort to exchange conversation more than anything else. I knew she wasn't a fan of its bitter taste or the caffeine.

"Thank you, *Filho*. But I'm jittery as it is," she answered, her eyes watching the window leading to the front gate, her fingers gently caressing the rabbit foot in her hand.

We had been sitting there for at least two hours, while the clouds shifted around the horizon and the sky changed into shades of crimson, purple and finally deep dark blue. I could see a light breeze traveling softly through the leaves of our tangerine tree outside, and it looked like it would be a mild December evening for a change. But for some reason there wasn't a soul outside.

I got up to walk to the kitchen to fix myself a bologna sandwich. My mother looked at me right as I was standing up, her eyes wide open, as if for a fraction of a second she thought I would know the answer to everything, as if I could've suddenly remembered that Pablo had some kind of commitment and wasn't going to be home until late in the evening, or that Pai had mentioned that he would take Pablo to finally get his hair cut.

"How about a sandwich, Mãe?"

She just closed her eyes and shook her head, disappointed.

It was almost ten at night when I finally saw my father hesitantly placing his hand on top of the latch to open our front gate. As he closed it behind him, he glanced back at the deserted street as if pondering whether or not he should go back out there again. He turned and walked to our front porch. Neither one of us moved at first, just watched as he took a seat by the wooden steps, not making it to our front door.

With his elbows resting against his knees, my father buried his face in the palms of his hands, and wept. I watched him weep, like I had never seen before, and noticed his whole body trying to fight its own spasms, until it finally gave in, and we could hear his sobs and moans through the shut window. I don't think my father had ever cried before. Not even when they took the mine. And he used to say that the mine was his whole life. I stood there watching almost in awe of this man, wondering who he really was and what moved him, until his sounds started to blend with my mother's, and I couldn't distinguish the two anymore.

"Oh, no!" she said in between sobs. "Oh, no!"

What I hadn't noticed was that at one point my mother had gotten up to open the front door for my father, but she must have stopped herself when she heard the sounds coming out of him, and her tired little body gave into our flower printed couch once again. "Oh, no!" She kept crying, resting her head on her palms just like he did. And suddenly I couldn't take it. Her. Him. I couldn't watch it any longer. I ran through our front door, past my father, over the brick path that led to our gate.

"Where do you think you're going?" he yelled. "You come…" His voice sounded shaky, yet still strong. But it vanished as I turned the street corner. I just ran, watching the cobblestones disappear beneath my feet, then the dirt road on a different street.

I wasn't sure where I was going, but somehow I ended up staring at that President's poster once again, waiting for it to come to life, so that I could fight it. He looked different in the night light. A trimmed mustache adorned his round face. The receding hairline made his forehead glisten more where hair used to grow, picking up on the shine of his pins and medals, and reflecting the camera's flash, and the light post. I still thought that if you only looked at his face, he didn't seem frightening at all. I could see him being anyone's father or grandfather. But now that seemed diabolic. He wasn't looking at whoever took that photograph, as if the person didn't deserve a glance, even if for a second. His whole body was slightly turned to the right. He seemed bothered by the idea of having to stop what he was doing to do something as silly as taking a picture. He had things to get back to. More important things.

The rest of the wall was covered with a white paint, a thin coat as if intending to show how things worked those days. Everything was done to set examples. Everything. Prof. Caetano was no different. No casualty was left without witnesses. No sermon preached to no sinners.

I eventually sat on a grassy patch by the edge of the sidewalk and waited for Pablo to show up and put his stamp on that wall one more time, like he'd done for the past two years. 'They won't shut you up, Pa,' I remember thinking, over and over. 'They won't shut you up'. I remained in the same position until about two in the morning. And nothing. No Pablo, and no anyone. I thought about leaving, about going back home, about listening to what my father had to say, about comforting my mother. But I just stayed there.

SEVEN

SOMEONE JERKED ME back and forth by my shoulders as I struggled to open my eyes. My father's calloused hands came at me like a creature's tentacles. He slapped me on the face, head, shoulders, and chest while crying, "You selfish, little… Damn it… How can you do this to us? Your mother…"

He kept smacking, and hugging, and crying. I could feel his tears, his spit hitting my face.

"How can you be so self-centered?" he demanded, his voice a deep baritone and out of control. And right then I pushed myself up.

"What!" I cried. "You were the one who brought us to this. You were the one who brought him here! This is all *your* fault! We shouldn't have left. You and your damn pride made us lose him."

Only after I was finished I noticed my father feeling the edge of the sidewalk, searching for a surface to sit on and I immediately regretted what I had said to him. But I'd said it.

I wished that he would yell at me again, call me ignorant, *um piá de merda*, and dismiss me because I didn't know what the hell I was saying, and because I didn't know anything.

The colors began to shift as dawn cut across the horizon, and a few people passed by us heading to their jobs, still half asleep as if nothing had changed, as if their world hadn't collapsed. Would life go on as usual even though Pablo had disappeared? Many sons had vanished and it didn't keep them from going on about their life. People walked, waited by their bus stop, let their dogs out to pee, and yawned, as if it was just another day, and the planet hadn't shifted on its axis. My father just sat there, watching his own feet.

"C'mon, Pai. Let's go home. Mãe must be worried," I said.

I wanted him to leave that wall. He didn't even know what it meant, and I didn't want to share it. I knew this about Pablo, and at that time, it was all I had.

My father got up, and we walked home in silence. Mãe was waiting on the same flower printed couch I had left her. Her body looked to have shrunk a few inches, and her eyes would barely open through the swelling of an entire night of crying; still she had a tender smile on her face. She looked at me, studied my body and caressed my face slowly and gently enough that I could feel her hands trembling.

"I'm so sorry, Mãe. *Desculpa*." I put my hand over hers.

"There's no need, *amor*." She fixed my hair. "Now you go get some rest. Maybe you'll wake up, and we'll all realize this was a bad dream." She forced another smile.

...

I walked into his room determined to find something that would lead me to where he was. I found his spray paint hidden under the bed, and I tried to wrap my fingers around its aluminum container. It was cold against the palm of my hand. The night I saw Pablo painting the wall, he held it with one hand only. But he had our father's hands, his fingers lengthy but strong from the carpentry work he'd done. I couldn't understand why he wouldn't take it with him wherever he was, and if it was possible that he quit the whole thing. But it sounded too good to be true, and not at all likely, based on what he had said the night before. But why would he leave it behind? Maybe he didn't plan on leaving. Maybe he was planning on coming back home and just never made it. There was a tightness in my lungs, and a knot in my throat as I tried my best to push that thought as far away as I could.

His closet seemed the same. I could recognize the pieces of clothing he wore the most still hanging neatly. His brown flannel shirt, for instance. I pulled it out of its hanger, and brought it to my face. His shirt smelled of smoke and lavender from all the sachets our mother used to spread around our closet and drawers. I grabbed its right sleeve and brought it close to my nose. What do tears smell like? Can we smell the salt in them? Does its scent fade in the course of only one day? What else can fade that quickly?

I shut the closet door and put Pablo's shirt on, all the while thinking I shouldn't be doing that. Maybe he would walk in at any minute and get mad at me for going through his room. With each button I touched, I understood my wishful thinking and allowed time to pass as quickly or slowly as it desired. Regardless of how fast or slow, all I wanted was to stay in place.

I sat on Pablo's bed, its mattress giving in a little, its checkered spread oscillating in reds, and greens, and blues. I wiped my face with Pablo's shirt, while I sat there watching his bedroom door as he had done the night before, waiting for Pablo to open it, to pause there for one brief moment for me to tell him how much I have always loved him.

How do we rewrite our lives?

I kept looking, hoping to find something different, something missing from that room. And the more I looked the less it made sense to me. I found four trash bags filled with marbles in his shoe closet, which was the strangest of all – not once had I seen him play with marbles, not even when we were kids. He'd never shown any interest in them when I played around the house. I wondered if I even knew who Pablo was, if it was possible that he wasn't this rebellious, fearless and mysterious person he seemed to have become. And if the message on the wall was just a fluke, done more as a payback for what happened at the mine. Maybe his secrets had nothing to do with the regime. He played with marbles, for Christ's sake.

Looking back now, I can't help but think they were all children, the rebels; those who did everything they could to give our country back to its people were all innocent and naïve in their quest. They had to be.

. . .

One rainy Sunday afternoon, while I was playing with marbles in the hallway back home, I kept tossing them with just enough force to have them go about a meter away from me and then come right back, as they succumbed to our house's incline. They never came back exactly the same. Some followed the creases in the hardwood floor, while others surfed them, picking up more speed. Pablo was bored from being stuck inside the house, and watched me play.

"Throw them harder," he said. "See if they'll pick up even more speed." He leaned back on the chair that sat by the end of the staircase.

I tossed one real hard and it hit the base molding at the end of the hallway.

"Luca, if you're going to play that way you will need to go outside," my father yelled from the family room, while Pablo mouthed his words, frowning, and hunching himself over on the chair to mimic our father. I covered my mouth to keep me from laughing too loud. And Pablo kept going, making it very difficult to remain silent.

I threw another marble, then another, then another, and followed them as they all came back to me. Then I threw a whole bunch of them, acting as a goalkeeper when they rolled back. Pablo laughed as I struggled to get them all. I played that game for a long time.

"We should play soccer once the rain stops," announced Pablo.

"Yes!"

I heard my father's footsteps somewhere in the house, but didn't notice they were coming towards the hallway, and I kept on playing. I threw all my marbles again, and while I waited for them to come back, my father stepped over me, wanting to get across. I can still remember this very clearly. My father's right foot surfing on two marbles. And as he struggled to maintain his footing, he stepped on a few more with his left. His entire body swung back then forward. The image in my head is that of a giant about to collapse over me in slow motion. And the only reason my father did not fall was because his arms were long and strong enough to hold on to the walls on both sides of the hallway. I almost ran away from him I was so afraid.

"Luca!" he yelled. "You are absolutely not to play with marbles here anymore! Do you understand?" His face was pink as he straightened his sweater. He looked like he would beat me just then. "It could have been your mother, for Christ's sake!"

"She's used to this, Pai. She always lets him know she's about to pass," Pablo said.

"Do I look like I'm negotiating here, Pablo?"

Pablo shook his head.

"I'm sorry, Pai," I said, hoping that our mother would let me play again on weekdays.

Our father left while I was still collecting all the marbles from the floor.

"Hey," Pablo whispered. "Sneaky marbles!" he mouthed, and we both laughed quietly.

...

His knees kept giving in and he almost collapsed each time one of them buckled. He stood against a white-coated brick wall, his hands tied in front of him. It smelled of feces and urine.

He studied his own hands. His fingers. His nails. Although dirty, they were still there.

An officer walked in and slapped him hard on the head. It swung from one side to the other as if he had no spine. His eyes were closed.

"What are you standing up for? I told you to sit down!"

He smacked Pablo again, but he didn't feel a thing. His head hit something or someone. That was when he noticed there were others in the room with him. Each prisoner took a seat on the disgusting floor.

Pablo touched his own head, his hair, his face. He was not

hurt. Just extremely exhausted. He'd been up for three days in that same room without food or water. He remembered being given an injection at one point. He has seen things. His own eyes can tell they have seen things which his brain can't quite process.

But somehow he knew what was coming. This was only the beginning. Was it their constant reminder, their constant harassment? Or did he understand where he was? But it felt good to sit down, and close his eyes for a brief moment.

The same officer slapped his head again. It swung left, then right. Elastic.

"What are you sitting down for? I told you to stand up!"

His legs were wet, covered in urine and dirt. They shook uncontrollably as he pushed himself up. For a moment it looked as though he wouldn't make it, as though his legs weren't his anymore. But he did. And he stiffened them in place, closed his eyes, and fell in a deep dark sleep.

Same officer walked in again. Slapped Pablo's head.

"What are you standing up for? I told you to sit down!"

Smack. "What are you sitting down for? I told you to get up!"

Smack. "What are you standing up for? I told you to sit down!"

...

It must have been noon when I woke up and realized I had fallen asleep in Pablo's room. His bed covers had little wrinkles from the weight of my body, but the room looked pristine otherwise. I sat on the bed remembering our last conversation, the way he tapped on the mattress, the way he looked into my eyes, the way he cried as I was leaving his room. I was convinced that he knew he was leaving us. I was convinced he had planned on hiding for a while, just until things calmed down, so that he could come back home safely.

But when I left Pablo's room, I was shocked to see that

pretty much everything in our house had been boxed up while I slept. All but Pablo's bedroom, which my mother started to organize as soon as I emerged from it.

"What's going on, Mãe?"

"Good morning, Luca." She didn't stop working to look at me.

"What is going on, Mãe?" I repeated, louder this time.

She glanced at me, but quickly turned the other way, as if avoiding something painful.

"We're moving, sweetie," she announced while folding some of Pablo's coats that hung in his closet. "Your father doesn't think it's safe for us to stay here."

"How is Pablo ever going to find us?"

She just looked at me, tears bursting out of her eyes, like she needed to yell as much as I had just yelled her. But she just didn't know how.

I left Pablo's room in search of my father. He was boxing up some books in the living room.

"Have a seat, *filho*."

He put down the books he had in his hands and took a seat across from where I was. His tired eyes looked as though they had each taken a punch. He cleared his throat.

"I know this seems crazy, but you need to understand what is happening," he paused, glanced at the front door. "We don't know what happened to Pablo yet. But if he was arrested, they will come here."

I stared at the front door while my father spoke, wishing that Pablo would just walk in and put an end to this.

"They torture people, Luca, to make them talk."

"I know. I heard." I kept looking at the door.

"And when they don't talk, they find their families to torture them too. They could take you or your mother, torture you in front of Pablo."

"They do all sorts of horrible things to people," he kept going. I was looking at him now. "And they don't care if it's

85

women or children at all. They'll torture a baby, if that's what it takes."

I remember finding that hard to believe.

"And when people finally talk, they don't need them anymore." He looked at his shoes for a moment. "Do you understand what I'm saying, Luca?"

I nodded. I didn't want to understand. But I knew our father was right. If we gave Pablo a reason to talk, they could kill him.

"I can't let anything happen to you or your mother." We were looking at one another like we hadn't done in a very long time and it was making me uncomfortable. I wanted to say something, but words escaped me.

"But what if Pablo comes to find us?"

"Rita will know where we are." Rita lived on the street below us, the one house my father had checked to see if Pablo could be hiding there. We didn't know any of his new friends. "She already knows he's missing."

...

The new house was about eight zigzagged blocks away. It was a bit smaller than the previous one, but they looked so similar to one another it made the whole move seem more surreal to me. On the outside, it was a fading yellow, with a green door and windows. I hated its patriotic colors, and was relieved when my father agreed that we should paint it sooner rather than later.

I walked down the hallway to where the bedrooms were and picked the smallest one for myself. It was the farthest from the master bedroom which would later come in handy for me. It was also next to what we thought would become Pablo's bedroom, and I liked the idea that we could share a wall again. Its parquet floors echoed more than in the other house, a familiar sound. We crossed it many times with our belongings, each time reminding me of Minas do Leão, of our hollow home.

My mother took it upon herself to pack and unpack

everything that belonged to Pablo, making sure all would go to its proper place, as long as the new house allowed. She didn't look at the rest of the house until she was done with his things. She just stayed there where his room was supposed to be, hanging his clothes, making his bed, fixing his bedspread. She placed the little lavender sachets behind his clothing, inside drawers, and under his pillow. She called me in.

"Luca, honey, can you help me with these bags? They are too heavy."

They were the four bags of marbles that were in his wardrobe. She didn't open them to see what they were. She had me place them exactly where I had found them the night before. Right below his brown flannel shirt, behind his shoes.

It was strange to watch her. As if only part of her was present, as if she found herself in a parallel world, one I wasn't invited to. She had seemed that way when we moved to Porto Alegre, when we boxed up our home. I hadn't realized it then. I thought that was how people reacted when they moved. They had too much on their minds. But I could see her in that bedroom, and I realized I had been wrong. It was the opposite. A good fraction of her mind seemed shut off then.

She asked my father to put Pablo's desk by the window, because it was the only place that made sense for it to be. But I could tell the rearrangement bothered her deeply. She pushed through the night. The second night without any sleep. My father had plenty of *cachaça* that evening. The first time I saw him drinking without any company, and at one point he passed out. The only sounds I heard were his snoring and occasional thump from Pablo's bedroom.

I grabbed my pillow from my new bedroom and went to Pablo's room.

"Mãe, is it okay if I lie down here while you work?" I asked. "I don't feel like being by myself tonight."

"Of course, *meu amor*," she said. "We'll keep each other company. Go ahead and get some rest. I'll try to be quiet."

I placed my pillow on the parquet floor and lay down next to Pablo's bed.

"Luca, you'll catch a *resfriado* like this. Take the bed!"

"No, this feels good. I like the floors here." I said, and Mãe continued to work.

My mother worked vigorously. The entire house remained a mess, but she didn't care. She went through his books and papers. She studied his handwriting, she caressed the paper to feel at which letters Pablo pressed a little harder, and which letters came easily for him. She found old candy wrappings forgotten between pages, inside pockets. She found a lighter and wondered if Pablo would have taken up smoking had my father stopped for good. She discovered many things about Pablo from these little forgotten trinkets. He hadn't changed as much as one would think just by looking at him, by sitting with him for a meal.

She did her best to remember how she had found all these things, how carelessly or carefully they had been placed where they were. She put them back where she thought they belonged, where it would make sense for Pablo, where he would want them. A few times she changed her mind about where something should go. She would sit on his bed and just study whatever it was, an old notebook, a drawing of a sunset, a broken pencil sharpener. She'd study them until she felt sure.

When everything seemed to be in place, she sat down on his bed again. Exhausted from the lack of sleep and food, from crying, from living this life which had become hers all of a sudden. She grabbed his pillow, taking half of it off of its pillowcase. It was old, and stained, but Pablo had always liked it and wouldn't let her get a new one. She hugged it and smelled it and kissed it and let her tears stain it even more and patted her face dry with it and covered it again and put it back in its place, fluffing it with care. She then got up, grabbed the piece of paper which had been in her pocket all day long, and put it back where she had found it. Under his mattress.

My mother made Pablo's room feel more like his than I was ever capable or willing to do with my own.

. . .

She stood by his nightstand watching the highs and lows of his protruding stomach beneath the yellow sheets while he snored loudly like he'd always done. Before all this she had found comfort in the way he snored. He was a big man, who carried many responsibilities on his shoulders, a hardworking man who would go to the end of the world and back to protect his family and their integrity, to do what was best for them. She liked how he could fall into such deep sleep as soon as he laid his head on a pillow. She thought he must've felt at peace with himself, that he had done his job that day and could rest assured, and so could everybody else in his home. And before all this, she felt the same way. She concurred.

But as she stood by his nightstand now, as she realized how easy it continued to be for him to simply shut down and let himself go into this deep serene sleep of his, how quickly his snoring escalated, as if his mind was clear, as if he owed nothing to no one, as if he wasn't a disappointment, she began to despise the sounds he made. She was suddenly angry at herself for thinking he wouldn't let anything get out of hand. She should've known better. Her own mother would have told her that.

The fact was that she had no doubt in her mind that she had failed. As a mother, she had failed. And it cost her more than she could ever afford. It wasn't all his fault and she knew that. But how he could possibly continue to sleep like that was one thing she couldn't understand.

EIGHT

MY FATHER MADE me take kung fu lessons three times a week. People had become obsessed with it since the first Bruce Lee movie came out, and boys and men walked around with homemade staffs like they knew what to do with them. Every Friday was match day at the gym; not a competition, but to showcase one's technique. My father would sit through these matches every week, his back straighter than I thought possible, his face almost that of a statue, frozen to the world, but there for me to look at.

On the night I was matched with Eduardo, we faced each other on the matt's center, clasped our hands together and bowed on the referee's cue. He was new in our gym, a tall seventeen-year-old, who had earned his yellow belt in less than a month.

As we locked eyes, I heard his family cheering for him from the bleachers. Different voices yelling his name excitedly, as if there was more at stake than one's honor.

"You got this, *filho*!" I heard a man's voice, then saw Eduardo blushing immediately after. He gave me a look of annoyance.

I glanced at my father, and found him in the exact same position, as if he hadn't blinked all this time. I wished he would just leave.

We put on a good fight, it was certainly one of my best fights, and eventually our instructor signaled to stop, congratulating us both on our progress.

Once these matches were over, my father and I would ride home in silence. All we'd hear was the rumble of his VW's motor and the monotone speech from the car's stereo covering what other brilliant measure our government had announced that day. Every evening at seven o'clock our ears were bombarded with propaganda. Only once in a while they would address the opposition, acknowledge the communists, terrorists spread across our country, contaminating those around them with subversive ideals, and they would remind us what was in it for them. My father would listen through it all without so much as a word. He would not talk about the regime. He would not say anything remotely related to the regime. Just like he never said anything about how he thought I did at kung fu, or anything else I was doing for that matter. All he did was tap my shoulder whenever it seemed to him as though I would've won and have a look on his face, which seemed to waver between relief and guilt.

. . .

We all had our theories of what we thought, and of what we believed each of us thought had happened to Pablo. I knew that my mother held on to the idea that he was hiding somewhere, waiting for a better moment to come home. She would leave snacks outside his bedroom window, in hopes that he would pass by someday and not resist. I'm pretty sure my father was convinced that he was dead, although he wouldn't dare say it. It was an objectivity he always said ran in the Fonte family, but I saw it as hopelessness.

I, on the other hand, thought that a combination of the two was probably what had happened, if that's even possible. Pablo became somewhat of a ghost to me. I couldn't picture him dead *or* alive. But he was out there somewhere, waiting for a change, for a proof that his choices weren't in vain.

His name was seldom spoken, and sometimes it seemed as though he never existed, except the weight of his absence loomed over us like a loaded storm. I'd lay on his bed and stay there, hoping the room would speak to me, hoping that resting my head where his had been would help me better understand him, would maybe change the way I thought and then lead me to where he could be. I'd waste hours there, going through his stuff, in an effort to find a clue he'd forgotten to burn. I would spend more time in his room than mine, usually falling asleep on his bed.

It was strange how much I could feel his presence in that room even though he hadn't set foot in it. I also learned a whole lot about my mother while I went through Pablo's things. She loved him without questions or judgment, enough to respect his incriminating clues. I wondered if she knew what they meant, if she even wanted to know, but I figured that she was more concerned that Pablo felt as though she respected his privacy, if he someday made it home.

I found a list of addresses under his mattress. A crinkled page from a notepad, folded in four, fuzzy at its edges. I thought of my mother placing it there, wondering if they would lead to Pablo, considering the idea of visiting each of these places, finding out what they were. I wondered if the list would make her scared or angry enough to want to just burn the piece of paper out of spite. Regardless of what she thought of it, it didn't keep her from returning it to its place.

I'd walk past some of these places every afternoon on my way back from school wondering what they meant. With Pablo's spray paint hidden inside my shirt, I was always trying to find him, to understand him, to *be* my brother.

I'm not sure what got into me on the very first time I walked by myself at night. I was sitting on my bed in this new bedroom, studying its walls. They held no secrets, they hadn't witnessed anything that could possibly help me understand what our lives had become. The light in my parents' room had been out for at least an hour, and I just grabbed the piece of paper with the addresses, his spray paint and jumped out of what should've been Pablo's bedroom window.

One of the addresses was Praça da Matriz, which was very close to our old house, a section of downtown I was somewhat comfortable walking around. Downtown was deserted and quiet in the evening; like a different place altogether. It seemed safer to be out at night, and I walked with ease. It felt good to be exposed to some of the things that my brother had seen. I'd occasionally hear a car speeding up as a traffic light turned green or as it turned a street corner. But otherwise, I was left with the coo of doves echoing through the empty streets, travelling from the rooftops of its tallest buildings or from the lowest windowsills.

Yes. There was a clear sense that I was out of my element. But that feeling, oddly enough, had become familiar to me. And I found comfort in its momentary legitimacy.

Stray dogs slept against garbage cans and by bus stops, not bothering to open their eyes as I walked past them, almost as if I were invisible. But that changed when I turned left onto Borges de Medeiros to take up the stairs. The stairway, which I'd taken several times, was too dark at night. Through the only burnt yellow light post working at about midway through it I could see the contours of scattered people laying against its rail, or the wall on the right. Homeless people slept along its sides, lifting their heads to watch me walk by, others half-asleep, but certainly awake, maybe drunk, surveyed me as I approached them.

"Go fuck yourself! *Seu filho da puta!*"

The sound came from Borges, the street I was on before taking the steps, and it was my cue to run as fast as I possibly could to Duque, to get the hell out of those stairs and get to that *praça* before I changed my mind.

Once I made it out of the stairway, I hit a corner *boteco*, which still had plenty of customers crowding the tables that took over the entire sidewalk. Each group so into whatever conversation was going on, they hardly noticed me as I made my way through the tables.

When I reached Praça da Matriz, there was a group sitting by the center fountain, smoking cigarettes. I took a seat at one of the benches and watched them from a distance. There was nothing suspicious about them. Nothing at all. I wondered if I'd recognize some of Pablo's friends; if they would recognize me. I was too far to hear anything they were saying, so I just observed their body language. Had they been Pablo's friends, could they have gotten in the habit of doing the same things that Pablo would do? Would one of them flick his head back to get his bangs out of his face? Would another put both of his hands in his back pockets then hunch over as if his spine was made out of rubber? Would any of them have any spray paint?

One of the guys reached for a girls' hand, and pulled her up until she stood. He led her through a very slow dance. They danced as if the rest of their friends weren't watching, the entire world shut off, as if they were alone. When they stopped, the guy gave her a kiss on the crook of her neck, and she backed away, as if tickled, smiling. The rest of the group clapped, and he bowed.

A black cat came to check on me and I hissed at it. It walked away with a resentful meow. My heart raced again, my cheeks burned, but before I could try to calm myself down, I noticed they were all standing up. They exchanged kisses and a few of them left. One man, or boy – they just looked like men because they seemed very comfortable in their skin – walked in my direction. We looked at each other, and he half-nodded. I wondered if he knew Pablo. If he knew him well enough to see a subtle trace of him in me, to make the connection.

When the place was clear, I walked up to the fountain. The base below had a fresh coat of paint, and I was positive this was one of the places where Pablo was supposed to write his message. I knew it. That was what the list of addresses was. They were the places where he left his stamp – public parks, bridges, walls across from libraries, the city hall... Now they were all covered with paint, and the same President's poster, which didn't look as crisp as it did the first time I saw it. It had crinkled and faded with the constant shifts in weather, which made it seem as if a fog covered its demonic features. I thought about tearing it up, and rewriting Pablo's words. Not because I necessarily agreed with my brother, but because I felt I owed it to him.

I touched the can I had tucked into the waist of my pants. It was cold against my fingers. Burning. But warm against my waist. I stood there watching that space, holding his spray paint still tucked to my side. But I was too afraid to pull it out, let alone use it.

...

My mother saw my father pace around the living room all afternoon, his forehead knit in a permanent frown. She observed him out of the corner of her eyes as she went about her daily duties, so that he wouldn't notice her. Three times she saw him digging through the basket by the fireplace, through its old newspapers. Three times she thought about starting an argument, but stopped herself. Slices of sunlight cut through the shut blinds, as dust specks joined my father's frantic dance. She could sense his suspicious eyes following her whenever she walked by on her way to the kitchen, or out the front door to finish cleaning the porch. She avoided eye contact as much as she could. She was determined to not give in. But at about 5pm she found my father digging through the fridge, moving things around, disturbing her order, disregarding her territory.

My mother huffed as she walked to their bedroom, where she would find inside the bathroom cabinet the bottle of *cachaça* she had hidden from him. She knew he would desperately look for this bottle like he'd only once done for her vanished son. She didn't expect to feel bothered by it. Holding that half-drunk bottle in her hand, she looked at herself in the mirror, the lines around her sunken eyes. She couldn't remember the last time she had fixed her hair, or worn any makeup, or the last time she had wanted to do those things.

She turned the switch off and walked back into the living room, picked up the old newspapers inside the basket by the fireplace, and set the bottle beneath them. My father was still poking around the fridge when she got to the kitchen. She stood behind him for a moment, watching his hands, his curved spine. Her husband's hands weren't the same either. They looked smaller, thinner, their knuckles swollen; all strength gone. She couldn't bring herself to speak to him, and my father was again oblivious to her presence.

She eventually pulled up a chair for herself. Its iron feet scraped against the tiles, startling him. He motioned toward the chair across from her, as if her sitting there were some kind of signal she was sending him, requesting his attention, his time. Maybe to work things out between them, and solve their differences, find a common ground. But she just gave him a quick nod then tossed her head to the right, toward the living room, and refused to look at him afterwards.

...

On the day my father discovered my poems he looked as though he was about to puke on them. We hadn't been talking much. No one had been talking much in our house. My father didn't wait until I got home from the university by the living room window as he used to with Pablo. He didn't choose an uncomfortable chair. He didn't keep a *chimarrão* in his hand to stay awake. He didn't go to campus after me to make sure I was staying out of trouble. He never even told me to stay out of trouble.

I had had a late dinner that night because I got held up with a group project. My father of course had already eaten, and Mãe had kept one plate of beef stew, rice and mashed potatoes in the oven for me. She poured me some water and sat across from where I was with a smile on her face. A frozen, closed-mouth smile unmatched by her eyes. As hard as she tried the look of sadness just never left her, making her own struggle that much more apparent to me.

"How is school, *filho*?" She used the dishcloth to dry her hands, and folded it neatly in front of her. She then, as a tic, patted the hair rollers underneath her headscarf, her hands veiny as a grandmother's.

"It's alright," I said. "I think college is even worse than high school. We don't really study anything true. It's all processed, all chewed up for us."

"I know. It's horrible." My mother sympathized with everything and everyone, it seemed.

We eyed each other and decided on dropping the subject.

"Antonio!" she yelled after a moment of silence. "Luca is here!"

She smiled at me and we both took unspoken bets as to whether my father would stop doing whatever it was that he could be doing to join us.

As expected, my father didn't come and both of us won.

"Thank you, Mãe," I said, placing my plate on the sink. Her daisies were still as perfect as when we moved to the city. She watched as I patted my hands dry on my pants. "It was delicious," I added.

"Come here, *filho*," she said. "I want to give you a kiss."

I approached her and stooped over, and she kissed my forehead.

"You get some rest, *meu amor*," she said as I left for my room.

The house was empty, and I couldn't smell the smoke from my father's cigarette coming from anywhere. When I got to my bedroom I found my father sitting on my bed with sheets and sheets of paper spread around him and across the floor. I'm sure he'd heard my footsteps across the hallway as I approached him, but he didn't flinch at all. His brows were arched in a way I hadn't as a child seen. He rested one elbow on his knee and stared at a sheet of paper he held in his hand as if he was learning something horribly embarrassing about his own family in the newspaper.

I immediately realized he had found all my poems. Gone through them. And in my delusional hope I was waiting for an apology.

"What do you think you're doing?" he asked. His eyes were fixed on the one poem he held in his hands.

"Me?"

"Don't you see what's happening to people?"

He shook the piece of paper as he said the word "people" and I knew exactly what he meant.

"I see," I said. "It's not like I'm showing this to anyone. No one saw them."

He looked at me, a look of despair.

"Well, no one except for you now," I said.

"So, what? Why do you do this?" He threw it on the floor. "Is that your plan to fight all this? In your room? Where no one can see?"

"It's not a plan. I don't have a plan. I can't fight." I looked down because I couldn't look at him, because I knew he thought I was a coward, and I had to bite my tongue in order to keep inside what I thought of him.

"It's not going to bring anybody back."

He smacked the one poem titled "Pablo" against the mattress and walked away, stepping on everything I had written so far as if they were the garbage stray dogs had managed to get out of trash bags, spread across our sidewalk and neglected.

"They were the heroes of their own illusion.
Their own flesh, their currency"

His shoes, heavy on the wood floor, left prints on most of my poems. I have kept them just like that.

...

The resistance movement grew stronger and more systematic as the years passed. Some even called it organized crime. Protests brought thousands of people out on the streets at significant dates – the anniversary of a reporter's death, the kidnap of an author's son, Independence Day... We would hear horror stories of what people went through, of how their house had been invaded by officers after some kind of clue, of people who died in protests, people who didn't survive the tortures they were put through, or others who were rumored to have escaped and fled to another country, or who became *clandestinos* inside our own. We would hear a whole lot, but nothing about Pablo.

Students wouldn't dare gather around the university campus. Instead, they planned their next steps during class. I sat as close to them as I possibly could, trying to blend in with the background, hoping that one day someone would mention my brother's name.

"It's at *aparelho*, I'll get it to you tonight after the game. Zeca has the key and I'm seeing him later," I heard João saying it, and I immediately remembered Pablo mentioning that word on his last night at the house.

João ripped a piece of paper from his notebook, wrote something really quick and passed it down to Gustavo, the guy he was whispering to before. We were all waiting for our professor who must have been running late, and I pretended to work on the poem I had in front of me. Gustavo looked at the note and put it in his pocket. Once class was over, I noticed him throwing some things in the garbage can before heading out. I waited for everyone to leave, then went through the garbage, but the paper wasn't there. This became a routine for me. I would watch everything and everyone and talk to very few people.

Whenever I managed to learn their whereabouts, I'd follow my classmates around and watch them talk from a distance. But I couldn't bring myself to join them, even though I wished to at least once feel what Pablo might have felt. I wanted to feel the rush of doing something dangerous, forbidden. I wanted to feel the power of believing one could make a difference. I wanted their hope more than anything in the world. I wasn't sure why I kept going back. I knew Pablo wasn't there. But these boys or men and these meetings quickly became my life. Almost every night, I'd jump out of his bedroom window, which became my bedroom unofficially, and with his spray paint tucked inside my shirt, I'd walk to where these meetings were taking place: behind a closed factory or a poorly lit public park, a random bus stop, a local *boteco*. Once the meetings were over, I would write 'They can't shut us up' somewhere they could see it, if these people ever returned.

The first time I wrote Pablo's message was on that wall close to our house, where I once saw him writing it. The same wall I had gone back to when I saw my father on the porch. That place was nowhere listed on that piece of paper. It wasn't a very public spot. But something had made Pablo put his stamp there. Was he training for the real deal, when he would be doing something forbidden at a completely exposed place, where someone could be watching him? Was he practicing the writing itself? He was a perfectionist whenever he built anything in the shed. Or maybe, he just did it for the heck of it, because he deeply loved the feeling of leaving his stamp, that when he headed home, he felt compelled to write it one more time.

I remember the way I trembled as I felt the can growing cold against my hand from the rushing paint. I could feel the heat of my own blood being pumped up, the burning of my ears, the electricity in my brain. The spray can and I were complete opposites. And as I watched the letters forming themselves on the wall, as I breathed its intoxicating fumes, and watched the paint drip down the concrete, I was sure that we somehow balanced each other out.

...

He went straight to the *aparelho* when he left school that evening. He knew that even the *aparelho* was becoming risky for him and that he would have to come up with another place sooner rather than later. At one point he had hated home. Despised the fact that no one, not even myself, seemed to understand him, to believe in him. But now he missed it more than he missed the mine, and the life he once had. He wished that he could sleep on his own bed, he wished that he could eat our mother's food, he wished that he could watch a soccer game with my father. His brain, blurry with all these misty thoughts, filled with nostalgia for a life he had chosen to let go.

He got off the packed bus one stop before his and walked to the place. The street seemed quiet enough, no strange cars except for a rusty Fiat 500 around the corner. The usual stray dogs and cats populated the block that was quickly becoming very familiar to him. All lights were off at the *aparelho* and he wondered for just a second if he had forgotten an appointment, and was meant to be some place else. With its eighteen tenants, he couldn't remember ever being in that house alone.

As soon as he walked in, before he could turn the light switch on, he felt someone pushing what seemed like a pillowcase, a burlap sack over his head while his hands were being cuffed behind his back. There must have been at least two of them, but he couldn't tell, because they were quiet as burglars.

Pablo was taken back out of the house and thrown in a car, which sped up almost as soon as the door shut. He assumed the driver must have waited there the entire time, and he wondered if it was the Fiat 500 he had spotted. The car smelled of sweat, ashtray and that awful stench, almost like a dirty wet dog reek, from when clothes take way too long to dry on the clothesline. All was quiet as the car made its rights and lefts. So many of them he gave up trying to guess which direction they were going. He suddenly remembered that that same afternoon he had picked up a piece of paper with the addresses of two other *aparelhos*. He would have to talk to whoever owned the places or had signed their lease, to see if they would take him. He thought of his *companheiros*, of all the people he didn't know yet, who would be exposed if these men got their hands on that piece of paper.

"What the hell is going on? Where are you taking me?" He demanded.

"Shut up, *piá de merda*!" someone yelled from the right. His head was pushed to the left, banging hard against the window. Two different men laughed out loud from each front seat, he could tell.

"Don't waste my energy just now. I'm saving myself for when we get to DOPS."

Pablo had met only one guy who had gotten out of the DOPS. Most people who were taken there were never heard from again.

He would soon learn what that place was really about. A place with secret tunnels, each of which lead to yet a new kind of torture. A place where the walls served not only for confinement but also to echo the wails of those within it, to hint at what awaited you. A place crowded with disgusting holes filled with people's excrements, because making them relieve themselves in front of everybody was demeaning and that's exactly what they hoped for. A place with no law, no rights, and no way out. If a person ever made it out, if he or she were lucky enough to survive it, they would become a lesser version of themselves, and a greater version of themselves in other ways. But never the same.

But what Pablo also realized in that exchange was that he had lucked out as far as the other people were concerned, his *companheiros*. The piece of paper was in his left back pocket, and his hands were cuffed on his back. He pretended to be in pain, and pushed himself farther left, farther away from whoever had hit him. Then he managed to pull the paper out of his pocket and squeeze it into the seat cushions. With his middle finger, he jammed it as far down as it could possibly go. He then inhaled what was supposed to be a deep breath of relief, which was quickly interrupted by the brakes' awful squeal as the car came to a full stop.

. . .

Mãe had given me one of my father's button-down shirts and the tie Pablo had worn for high school graduation. It was hot as hell, but she insisted I'd dress up for the job interview, even though it wasn't all that important.

Downtown was crowded with the usual pedestrians and what looked to be a peaceful protest. The sun radiated through the buildings, reflecting from glass façades. A group of people walked down Borges de Medeiros towards Guaíba, holding up signs, demanding salary raises for secondary teachers who had been on strike for almost a month then. They held signs with the percentage they believed to be fair, with the number of days children had been out of school, listing the salaries of other government positions. Within the picket line, you'd see a couple of signs demanding autonomy of curriculum, and freedom of speech. Dozens of officers stood by to make sure all would stay under control.

I turned right onto Borges and followed them down to Rua da Praia. This was the intersection where most people circulated at any given day in Porto Alegre, and it was quickly becoming the place for all protests. It would soon be called The Democratic Corner. To this day, it still is. I got as close to them as I could, trying to make up what some of them screamed over the megaphone, trying to scan their faces for anyone I might recognize. My shirt was damp from the setting sun hitting straight into my face, and I stopped to fold up the sleeves of my father's shirt, when I saw Rita in the midst of them.

Rita had on a denim skirt, flip-flops, and a colorful flowered shirt. Her hair was up in a bun, and she was tan; a beautiful sight among such chaos. I hadn't seen her since the time she came looking for Pablo, and I had forgotten just how beautiful she was. There was something very comforting about her presence. As if she knew that in the end everything would be all right.

"Hey, Rita!" I yelled.

"Luca, *guri*!!! Man, you're a grown man now!" Her smile was inebriating. I was sure that I hadn't seen such an honest smile in years. "What are you all dressed up for?"

"Oh, this." I pinched my tie. "Job interview. How are you? You look so…"

"Cool, man! How did it go?"

"Good," I lied. I had changed my mind right then about making that appointment. "What are you up to?"

"Well, you know… doing my part." I couldn't get over just how ethereal she looked.

"Hey, do you want to have a Coke or something?" I asked.

She glanced back at her peers, and then shrugged. "I'd love to. I can come back later."

We took a seat at one of the stools in the first *boteco* we found. We could still see and hear the protest from where we were. We ordered our sodas and drank most of it in one gulp.

"Wow! So how are you? I haven't seen you in so long! Are you in college now? You must be, right? I feel like the last time I saw you must have been that day in your house. How is your mother? How is she holding up? Have you had any news, you know?"

Her voice, the way she looked me in the eye, the way she tapped my shoulder when she talked, the way she cared. Everything about her felt like home.

"I'm talking too much, right Luc? *Desculpa*. Go ahead, you talk."

She pretended to zip her lips with her fingers, and waited for me to say something.

"We're doing good. I'm studying literature…" I looked back at the crowd outside, then at Rita. "Aren't you scared? After, you know?"

She shrugged again.

"I have to do something. It's how I sleep at night."

I didn't sleep all that much anymore.

"My mother told me that you're writing poems now. What kind of poems do you write?" she asked.

Mãe had never spoken to me about my writing. But she had told Rita's mother about it.

An officer walked in and ordered a beer. He had his uniform on, gun in hand, he was clearly assigned to watch the protest. Rita glanced at him then rolled her eyes at me. The bartender poured him a glass.

"*Não!*" he barked, "*Sem colarinho!*" Then the bartender threw it out, and poured the officer another glass. No white foam, this time.

The officer downed his beer, then let out an "Ahh" afterwards, leaning back onto the counter as he watched the movement outside. And as he leaned back I saw, hanging on his neck, peeking out of his unbuttoned shirt, a golden necklace, with a São Jorge pendant hanging from it, just like my mother's. Just like Pablo's.

"Luca, what's wrong?" Rita whispered to me. "Stop staring."

"His necklace." I whispered back. Rita turned to look, then back at me. Her smile had left her. She was as white as I must have been. Her eyes watery.

Of course this could all have been just a coincidence. A São Jorge pendant was very common, especially for men. But looking at this officer, who must have been only a few years older than Pablo, it seemed pretty clear that he didn't seek protection, but instead he carried it like a trophy, a proof of his dominance, a reminder of his power. For me, it was everything I feared in life, everything that was wrong about the world. It was that forever-open wound. The one that just can't heal. Even if scars will form on the surface, they were, by nature, superficial and fragile. One can't not know what has happened to his vanished brother and pretend to be whole, to have that integrity.

"It could be just a coincidence." I said, trying to believe in it myself. "It's pretty common, I think."

"Yes." She agreed. She rubbed her hands against her face. "Let's go. Let's get out of here."

I paid for our sodas, and we left immediately. I wanted to apologize to her. She was happy before I saw her. Her smile had been sincere. I was the shadow she didn't deserve.

"I'm sorry, Luca," she said as we had gained some distance. "These people. They are not worth the shit they make."

"Have you heard anything? Anything?" I asked.

"I know he got pretty involved. I know that. He told me that on the last time we saw each other. He told me that would be the last time we'd see each other for a while."

She held my hand.

"Did he tell you how long that while would take?"

She shook her head.

"I don't think he knew. I don't, I don't know what happened to him, Luca. I'm sorry."

"Yeah. Me, too."

We hugged, and she told me she would get back to the protest.

"Don't be a stranger, okay? Let's do this again some time."

I nodded. "You be careful," I said.

She kissed me on the cheek. "Don't you worry about me!"

For most of my life I felt as though I didn't really exist, but was close enough to being real that people wouldn't notice it. The man I should've been just never became a reality. I felt as though I'd just hover over the people I knew, like the undead. I'd hover over them, and I'd hover over the memories I have of them and of myself, of this man I should have been. Memories from a future that just never came. Like a noon shadow. So close to the real thing that you can't identify where you end and the shadow begins.

NINE

THE ORANGE CURTAINS of her bedroom window were slightly open, allowing a slit of the late afternoon sunlight to infuse her room with different shades of apricot and peach and tangerine. Rita watched her reflection in the vanity mirror as she sat on her bed.

Her thin, delicate arm still hurt from her encounter with the officer on her way out of class that afternoon. Her heart was still stuck somewhere between her throat and her stomach. She looked at the reflection of the bruise he had left on her right arm, and could almost recognize the guard's four crimson fingers. She studied that mark thinking of how it had changed things, how it had changed her. She then looked at her messy ponytail and remembered how the officer had grinned when he called her a *princesa*, how he caressed her hair, and how he immediately pulled hard on that same ponytail, exposing her neck and collarbone as he swore he'd come after her if he discovered she was hiding her scumbag boyfriend from him. His other hand tugged tightly at her neck. By the way he had looked at her, the angry hunger she had seen in his eyes, she had no doubt their encounter could have been a lot worse, had he caught her in some deserted street somewhere. Inside her bedroom now, she tilted her head back and studied what her collarbone looked like, remembering the officer's face, waxy with sweat, the lust in his eyes.

It had been weeks since she'd last seen Pablo. Each day that he didn't knock on her window confirmed her fear that she would not see him again. She knew he was changing, she knew she was losing him, she understood his love for this cause was stronger than whatever he felt for her.

How stupid she had been for believing she could lure him back by giving herself to him. How naïve she was for thinking she could somehow enthrall him, as if casting a spell with her body and what could become of it, if they both gave themselves to each other. How silly to think he would give everything up for her. Just for her.

When they made love she thought his scent would never leave her skin, she thought she would never forget the way his lips felt on hers as he lay on top of her. How helplessly her voice had slipped into a falsetto as he had kissed breathy kisses on her neck. Behind her ears. On her belly. How softly his mouth had explored the back of her knees. His cologne no longer seeped through her skin. Her skin had no memory. These memories were in her head only. Her neck no longer remembered how cold his tears had felt as they slid through to her nape. Her whole body, gradually forgetting, as it discovered other ways it could be touched.

. . .

The light in my parents' room had already been out for hours when I left. I wore Pablo's brown plaid shirt for the first time outside the house that evening even though it was too hot for it. But I liked how fitted it was, how I felt more like a man in it. The shirt had already been washed several times by my mother along with every other piece of clothing of his, and it didn't smell like him. It smelled clean, but it still felt as though he was with me, guiding me through the streets, teaching me when to avoid eye contact with a passerby, when to look at a person in the eye, what I should search for when I got to one of these meetings – a spot to hide, one to avoid, a way to escape.

I walked through the empty streets listening to the buffered noise of television sets, watching the vibrating lives inside fenced houses. All security shutters on businesses had been pulled down, and rusty locks were properly engaged. No one wandered outside after dark. The only life you'd see were the animals' napping here and there, the homeless passed out asleep from alcohol, an occasional couple striding along, so in love with each other, reality becomes nothing but a background. I looked at the linear trail the telephone wires created along the sidewalks, the loose way with which they hung from the poles, pulsating at the sounds of coded conversations, disconnected dialogues, of secret nicknames, of desperate brides, of mothers' wails, of disappointed wives. Every once in a while a bird would take flight as if suddenly expelled from that particular wire, as if whatever it was transmitting had suddenly become too painful.

I got to the place about an hour before the arranged time. It was a cobblestone street that ended at a brick white-coated wall a little less than two meters tall. The full moon reflected off these cobblestones as if they had been waxed and polished all afternoon. A warehouse sat at the street's very end. Its banner was lit by two burnt yellow lamps, which served more for gathering clouds of various insects than featuring its own name. One of the lamps flickered every once in while. The words on the banner were fading and the only thing I could make out were "and Sons," which I thought was ironic. I stared at the brick wall, imagining Pablo's words there once they were all gone.

I walked around trying to find somewhere close enough to eavesdrop. I was sweating under Pablo's shirt, the spray can I had tucked into my waist was slipping down my side. There was a car parked about a hundred meters from the wall. A thick layer of dust covered the entire thing, and someone had written on its back window what looked to be "*ABAIXO A DITADURA*" and a "WASH ME" right below. But it was already being buried under even more dust. Three of its tires were flat, making the entire car sit lower, and all of it made for a decent hiding place. Except it didn't feel close enough. I went around the block to the other side of the wall. If they stood where I thought they would, I would be closer than I had ever been.

I sat on the ground with my back against the wall and waited as sparse clouds shifted across the night sky, the wall's muddled cemented seams poking at my back. I could make out what looked to be grassland, and I remembered how I had found Pablo many years before sitting behind the shed with a cigarette in his mouth as he looked at the mine. I can still see very clearly how he squinted his eyes, and pinched the cigarette with his thumb and forefinger, how he looked like a different Pablo all of a sudden. It was almost as if he demanded an explanation from the mine itself, as if he felt betrayed by it. If I ever had the curiosity of knowing what it was like to smoke a cigarette, it was that moment. I waited for these people to show up, imagining what the smoke would feel like in my throat, how it'd circle around my lungs, whether it would come out of my nostrils or my mouth. I pinched my thumb and forefinger wondering how the cushiony filter gave in to their pressure, as I tried to understand what had compelled him.

. . .

His toes and knees dug into the brown arid earth while his elbows rested on a big rock and he took aim. But he just couldn't take his shot because his hands wouldn't stop shaking from cold, hunger and all around weakness. It was their fourth day of training and even though his lungs had adapted to the high altitude, his body couldn't seem to acclimate to the cold in the Andes. It was a kind of cold he hadn't yet endured. Minas do Leão was nothing compared to this.

He pictured his vessels constricting, and his own blood thickening within his veins as each movement became more laborious. His eyes, moist from the sharp gusts of wind and exhaustion. Pablo was sick of all of it. He didn't want to go through this training. He didn't believe they could make it back to Brasil; he didn't think they had a chance. The clothes and shoes they wore were not at all appropriate for the climate. The guns they used were so old and rusty he was afraid they would kill the shooter instead.

The night before at camp, Zé had complained his feet hurt. That it was unbearable. Zé had finally stopped shivering, and his skin looked about three shades lighter than Pablo remembered, but no one but Pablo seemed to care. And when he finally took Zé's shoes off, the guy's right foot was all black, along with every toe on his left.

"C'mon, this is ridiculous! What's the point? He's gonna lose his feet!" Pablo whispered a little too loud to Ernesto, who spent his days acting as though he was the group's leader. Ernesto, such a cliché.

"No! I can't lose my feet!" Zé yelled in desperation and started bawling like a child.

"Just shut the fuck up the both of you!" Ernesto's eyes were fuming. "I can't help it if he can't take it."

"That's it. I'm leaving!" Pablo announced and started to collect the few things he had brought with him.

But it was too dark out, and he knew he would get lost. He eventually gave in and lay down next to Zé, his legs over the guy's feet in the hopes of making it better. Later, when everybody else was asleep, Zé poked Pablo and said he wanted to push through, that they only had two more days to go, and that they should stay.

Crouching behind that rock now, Pablo wondered if he would ever feel what it was like to sleep in his own lavender scented, starched sheets again. He wished that he could have just one more chance of waking up to the scent of our mother's beef stew heating up in the kitchen, to the sound of her footsteps across the hollow hardwood floor, or her sweet whispered voice as she caressed his hair and announced breakfast was on the table.

But several people had risked their lives to help him out of the country. And several others had risked their freedom in Chile to hide him. Along with his partners, Pablo was a revolutionary. A hero. A communist. An agitator and a subversive. This was what was expected of him. Guerrilla training in the Andes. Except no one really knew what they were doing. And most days they just fought amongst themselves.

But they had a debt. They hadn't been helped so they could

get to Chile and go on vacation. Their country needed them and him more than they needed comfort or safety. Most days Pablo saw those around him as lunatics. Fanatics. Holding on to ideals because they had nothing else to hold on to. Because most people they knew had died, because everything they had was lost, and because they needed something. Anything.

The view from the mountains was like nothing else he'd ever seen. The blinding snow, the dark brown earth beneath it, not quite as dark as back home, but close enough to make him pick it up and smell it with the hopes of detecting just a hint of sulfur. He liked the way the clouds sat in a valley, as if hiding. His world was more vast than he had ever imagined, yet he felt as confined as when he spent six days in someone's garage waiting for his ride to Uruguay. Each day they climbed a little further up, only to find yet another peak. And each time they conquered more territory, his partners would brag and yell they were heroes, survivors, that they were on top of the world, but Pablo thought he was at the very end of it.

While they hoped to go back and fight with even more vigor, while they fantasized about making it into history books, becoming legendary, the next Che, Pablo wished that he could just move on. He was done. He wished that he could speak Spanish well enough to blend in, that he could find himself a job, maybe at a local coal mine, or anything to busy his mind and keep him from thinking of home as much, so that he wouldn't miss us the way he did, wouldn't wonder whether or not Rita missed him, and how different their lives could've been if only he'd stopped when she asked him to.

...

Little by little, the voices I had been waiting to hear started to speak to me.

On the other side of the wall, they talked about all the things we had been taught to avoid.

"Last time I saw Joca he told me about a shipment. Said it was to be delivered at a farm in Bagé."

"Guns?" another voice asked.

I didn't catch any answer.

"Where from?"

"A base in Rio. Someone from the inside."

They must have been leaning against the wall as well, as I could almost hear their breaths.

"Were you guys talking about Joca? Our Joca?"

No answer.

"Do we know if he's still alive?" A girl's voice this time.

"No way to know." A different male voice. "But I heard there's an operation taking place. A group from Rio. I can't say which though. They are going after some gringo, and they have a list of *companheiros* they plan to exchange for that gringo's life."

"No kidding? *Verdade?*" A different girl.

"Joca's made the list," he announced very matter-of-factly. "I think there are more people from here in it, too. They haven't shown me the names. But I'm working on it."

They went on about organized protests that were taking place throughout the country, about bringing in ex-police and marine officers who were fired for not complying with military demands. About freeing jailed friends. I tried to imagine what jail was like, if any of them even knew what it was like. I tried to picture my brother in one of them. I wondered if inmates were dressed in uniforms, what they were served on tin plates, what they did all day. I kept hoping they would name these people they were risking their lives for, but all they mentioned were nicknames, most of which didn't make sense to me.

"I don't know, man. I don't know," said one of the voices, couldn't be more than twenty years old. "Who knows if Joca, Paco, Saci are still alive? What if we do all this and they're dead?"

The word Paco brought a rush of heat to my face. Paco could easily be Pablo's nickname. Maybe it was too easy. But I was still taken with a sense of hope.

"Man, all we're making is noise. We make nothing but noise. And it's not taking us anywhere. In fact, it's killing us all. They are taking us one by one, and we just keep on making noise."

A mosquito kept buzzing around my left ear.

"There is no other way, man. It's as simple as that," affirmed another. "It will just go on forever, unless we show them how far we're willing to go."

Their fears led to a discourse about duty. I listened from the other side of the wall. It sounded like there were about six of them. At one point I heard a female voice and wondered if it could possibly be Rita's. I could hear everything; their voices, their ideals, and their dreams. But I couldn't see their faces. I decided to run around the block and find a place where I could actually see these people. I managed to reach the parked car without being noticed, and crouched behind it.

Pablo's spray paint poked my ribcage as if to remind me that I shouldn't feel too comfortable in situations like this. But I wasn't comfortable. I feared they would spot me somehow, and think I was a spy, and that would be the end of me. I was sweating under Pablo's shirt.

The group I was listening to consisted of six men and two women. All at the very end of that street. Some sat by the sidewalk, two of them paced back and forth, and others stood leaning against that same wall, and I was surprised by how close we had been to each other. One foot, at most.

With the help of a burnt-yellow lamp hanging from a closed factory across the street from the warehouse, one of the men read the revoked constitution aloud with a rhythm usually saved for poetry, while the others smoked their cigarettes, listening, and nodding from time to time. They were no longer talking about guns, jail.

"Declaration of Rights," he announced.

The young man paused to smoke, then removed his hair from his eyes. One of the girls slapped her shin, immediately scratching it afterward.

"Article 131. *All* Brazilian citizens over eighteen years of age who register according to the *law* are electors."

The others nodded. Two of them stared at nothing, blowing smoke.

"Article 141," he continued, his voice a little louder. "The manifestation of thought shall be *free* and *without censorship*. The publication of books or periodicals does *not* depend on the approval of any public…"

I suddenly sensed something coming from down the street. It sounded like clacks against the cobblestones, maybe a chariot. The sound was quickly becoming louder and clearer and at one point I had no doubt the clacks were the horseshoes striking against the street, the stones. My hands trembled as I searched the ground for a stone or a broken branch, something I could use to warn them. Underneath the car I found a piece of a broken brick, and quickly threw it at the group of young men, then crawled back behind the car. The brick was old and dry, and it broke into a million pieces as soon as it hit the stone pavement. Its powder formed an orange cloud above it. One of the boys put his cigarette out and started walking towards me. His frail body was as thin as Pablo's. He wore a beige short-sleeve button-down shirt and shorts and flip-flops, and he conquered the pavement with both fear and determination. Once he was close enough, I grabbed his neck and pulled him to the ground. He looked like he could be fifteen, although his weary eyes reflected all the ugliness he must have seen, all the jadedness he carried with him.

Five men on horses turned the street corner. The buttons and pins on their uniforms gleamed in the moonlight, as their bodies bounced with each stride. Their guns also flickered on their sides, but as was the custom they had chosen their batons for that particular night. They held them up as flags.

With one hand covering this boy's mouth, I used the other to point at the approaching men. He immediately reached for his shirt pocket, pulling out a handful of glass marbles. A few

115

slipped from his hands bouncing on the sidewalk beneath us, disappearing underneath the abandoned car. The ones he could still get his hands on, he quickly recovered, as if they were gold. My eyes were fixed on that boy's unsteady hands, reaching for other pockets, all filled with marbles. And his eyes were that of terror, as he threw some at his friends.

As soon as the group spotted the ambush, two boys tried to jump over the wall but gave up midway through it. They all looked at one another for a moment. One of those instances when time seems to be meaningless. When everything stops. Their eyes were as big as the moon above us.

"This is it!" said one of them.

"Shit. Shit, shit, shit, shit," vented the boy next to me.

As the horses approached the car, he threw most of the marbles on the street right in front of us.

Marbles. This was their weapon.

Coming from us and the other boys, they bounced on the cobblestones like an insect army you'd see in cartoons. At first you could listen to the sound of them clacking against the stones, as if forming a luminous energy field. Everything electrified. And then, there was chaos, and all you could listen to was the storm inside our heads.

The two black stallions leading the pack were the first to lose their balance, and tremble. It was enough for their men to wobble unsteadily on top of them. One dropped his baton in midair trying to hold on to his horse's neck. But when the horse jerked as if to get rid of his man and save himself, he fell backwards about two meters away, his helmet hitting hard against the stone ground.

Meanwhile, the other three horsemen headed toward the trapped group, who continued to empty their pockets. A sea of marbles covered the pavement. One of the officers lifted himself as if riding on a horse track, as if racing to a finish line. His horse followed his commands, and when it stepped on the first marble that had landed on top and not in one of the cracks of the cobblestones, it stumbled and tripped more than the other two. With almost its entire weight shifted to its front legs, and with the officer's weight up to his neck, that stallion's front legs staggered and bucked. Its man tried to stay in place as the horse struggled but shifted further up the animal's neck. The horse finally landed on its shoulders on top of the officer's leg, bent inward, in what seemed to be a slow-motion shot from a western movie. The officer wailed in pain.

I couldn't believe my eyes. These boys were being hunted for fighting for the constitution, for demanding freedom, and were deemed terrorists for defending themselves with *marbles*. Where were these guns they were talking about?

I suddenly realized that I was alone. The boy was running toward the fallen officers. But as he kicked one of them, he was hit by the other's baton in the back.

"*Filho da puta!*" the officer yelled, as he continued to beat him mercilessly.

The other boys and girls fought the remaining guards. And the two groups were merging together, steps away from me. I had to do something. Pablo would've wanted me to do something. I grabbed his spray can from inside my shirt and headed for the fight. My heart pounding so fast I couldn't think straight. All I saw were the two against the one. The one boy who had been next to me. The two soldiers against him. I grabbed Pablo's paint and aimed it at the officer's face.

The officer yelled "Son of a bitch!" and swore to break every bone in my body as he shook his head back and forth in an effort to dodge my brother's ink, until he just shut up. Everything must have happened very fast, but I saw his face gradually becoming darker and darker with the moist ink. For a second he seemed to want to scream more, to threaten me, but the moment he tasted the bitter fumes again he shut his mouth and his eyes. The paint coated his eyelashes and mustache, and dripped from where his sideburns should have been. His entire face was pitch black when I stopped, and when he opened his eyes, his eyeballs looked even more devilish than before.

Meanwhile the skinny boy was going at it with the other officer. And for that brief moment, it looked like a fair match, as though we had a chance of victory. As though there was a 'we'.

"Run!" cried the boy. "Go get more people! Go!"

I did what I was told. I ran. I looked back once and saw the two groups getting closer to each other. I ran around the block, then past the intersection where I would hit a bigger avenue. My heart beating up against my throat as every part of my body shook uncontrollably. I don't think I had ever been as afraid as I was on that evening. I walked those empty streets afraid of my own shadow as it shifted on the ground with the scattered lampposts, wishing I could just give up on them and go home.

There was no one around anywhere. All I saw were closed commercial buildings, a few stray dogs digging through trash, a passed-out homeless man and his malnourished cat. The few homes there were had their lights off, their windows shut, their doors and gates locked.

I should not have left them. I'd never find any help around. That boy must've known that. He must have thought I wasn't meant to be there, and that I would not go back. I shouldn't have listened. I ran back as fast as I could. My heart racing, my limbs still shaking, and Pablo's paint bouncing, when I stepped in one of the cracks of the cobblestones. The side of my shoe got stuck and my ankle bent and my leg gave in as I fell with an excruciating pain. How pathetic I was. I sat there and promised to myself I'd never do this again. I had no business being involved with these people.

Once again I thought about going home, but they still needed help, even if mine. I got up and limped back to that street as quickly as I could, which wasn't quick at all. My ankle throbbed with each step, sweat streaming down my face. The whole walk back, I hoped to find at least one person around. Someone better than me. Someone to help them. Anyone. But nothing. And when I got to that street again, there was nobody there either.

The horses were gone, the officers were gone, and the boys and girls had also left. There was blood splattered on the stones, there was the black ink close by. Their marbles rested on the curbside and in between the cobblestones, like little forgotten treasures. As if the children had been called inside by their parents and forgot to clean up after themselves.

I sat on the sidewalk, and picked up the marbles around me. They were cold against the back of my hand. I let them roll around and eventually fall back to the street, and find their little nooks in between the stones. I thought about the bags of marbles I had found in Pablo's closet, and wondered how many times he'd had to use them, if any.

I glanced at the cobblestones stained with black ink and noticed some of the painted marbles in between them. Not exactly opaque, but a different kind of shine. I grabbed a couple of black marbles, let them roll on the back of my hand, and saved them in my pocket.

I wished I hadn't left them. I wished that I had fought with them. But it was too late. There were no clues of victory or defeat, only paint, blood and marbles. I walked over to the wall that had separated us before, and stared at it for a long time. How much longer could I keep doing this? What was the point? Would these or other people ever meet here again? Still I wrote, "THEY CAN'T SHUT US UP" on the wall that had trapped these students.

From that night on, I too carried marbles in my pockets.

. . .

My ankles are tied to an iron chair's rusty legs; its rough surface continues to poke through the cuts and gashes already left on my skin . My wrists are locked to its bare armrest. I'm completely naked and feel something pinching my testicles, but it seems as though I have been here long enough that all sensations have become blurred. A man dressed in a white gown is examining

119

me. He listens to my pulse and nods to his partner. "Motherfucker!" The other man spits, missing my feet. I watch him walk towards me as if I'm floating above them all, and realize Pablo was the one who had been on that chair all along. How come I can't feel my testicles? The man walks toward Pablo with marbles in his hands. His strut is manic. Pablo seems on the verge of passing out. The man starts to frantically shove marbles up Pablo's nose. I see two go in each of his nostrils and start screaming as I feel them crushing my septum. He covers our mouths with his bare hands, and we can no longer breathe. The sound of cartilage tearing to pieces seems to come from the very center of our brains.

I see the veins on your neck bulging, fighting for more oxygen. I see your eyes turning blood red. I see your fingers gripping the chair as if the chair itself could save you, could bring life back into your naked body. I see your naked body, and it's so frail and heroic. I see you, accepting your fate. You don't see me.

TEN

PAI WAS DIAGNOSED with lung cancer and spent the next two years bedridden, giving my mother something to occupy her mind, reasons to stay in the house and the freedom to leave whenever it suited her. He wasn't exactly a burden to anyone, but that winter was very hard on his body. By the end of May he was sick enough to not get out of bed at all.

My mother cleaned the entire room every other day, shaved him twice a week, and sponge-bathed him daily. My father would sometimes complain to her, beg her to leave him alone, saying he didn't want to be bothered that day, that he was tired, arguing that it wouldn't make a difference. But it did. It made a huge difference for her.

My mother also made me visit with him every day. At first, I would just sit there and watch TV with him, or listen to the radio, or sometimes just stare at the walls. The dark room reeked of naphthalene and dismay. But towards the end, I actually looked forward to our time together. The disease had softened him, and by the end we were pretty close.

"Pai, did you hear Inter hired Manga from Nacional de Montevideo? I heard he's really good."

"*Sim*. Supposed to be one of the best goalies in South America." My father's body was almost imperceptible underneath the beige lamb wool blanket, which was up to his neck. He tried not to move much, as it'd usually lead to a coughing fit.

"Bet we can win the *Brasileirão* next year! With Figueroa and Manga, nobody will get through our defense."

The radio hummed in the background.

"At least we'll put on a good fight."

He glanced at me; his facial features had softened too. The harshness I had grown used to and always identified with manhood gave way to what seemed to be fear and doubt, but mostly regret. As awful as I felt about it then, it made it easier for me to be around him.

"I can take you to the stadium some day. Maybe when the weather warms up again," I said.

"*Não, filho*, not for me. I'm fine with my radio." He forced a smile and was seized with a coughing fit, holding onto the bed with one hand and to his chest with the other.

I grabbed the little plastic bowl my mother had left on the bedside table and placed it close to his mouth as I patted his back. He eventually got a hold of it then hacked and spat up phlegm and a little blood, wiping his mouth with the white cotton handkerchief he had always carried with him, yellowish then like an old photograph.

I helped him lie back down, tucked him in, sweat collecting at his temples, and told him I'd be right back with a clean bowl.

"Thank you, *filho*," he whispered in his cigarette voice as I left the room.

My father died of pneumonia on July 1974. Eight years after he walked away from his job at the mine.

"I think he would want to be buried in Minas do Leão," I told my mother. "Or maybe cremated. His ashes we could spread at the mine. He'd like that."

We were sitting in the living room which we had reclaimed once my father became too ill to leave the bedroom. She watched the front window and the life outside its transparent curtain, as if all she wanted was to get up and walk for days.

"He wanted to come here, *filho*. It's where we should bury him." Her voice was stern.

The sky was heavy with clouds, and the air moist, the day unusually warm for July. The trees were restless as the breeze brushed through them, announcing the coming storm. Loose leaves wisped in the circling wind, as if calling on the clouds above. As my father rested before us, two large *urubus* glided aimlessly almost directly above our heads. Like thieves, accelerating his body's decay. Lightning struck on the horizon, then a few seconds later, we both heard the earth's rumble.

My mother stood very erect, solid, empty. I wanted her to cry so that I could console her. But she seemed all dried up.

"I hope it rains," my mother said.

"*Sim.*"

"I hope it rains for days." Her voice showed exhaustion and something else I couldn't quite grasp.

"Me too, Mãe."

I held her hand.

"Should we say a prayer?" I offered.

"I think I've prayed enough." Her eyes were fixed on the grave next to my father's.

How neat is death; a book is finished, we carry on with our lives. It changes us, and we see why. Life is never the same, but it is yours, it is you. You survive it. Next to my father's grave was someone called Giuseppe Moro He died young. Same age as Pablo when he disappeared.

. . .

My mother would move back to Minas do Leão soon, but before she did, she helped me set everything up in a room we had rented. It was at a pension for students downtown called República da Dona Anita. The place was an old well-kept brick building covered by a glossy coat of gray paint, located on Rua da Praia, close to the public market.

"*Solo un secondo!*" we heard as soon as we knocked on the door.

Dona Anita was the manager. A lively, slightly deaf woman in her sixties, whose Portuguese was almost constantly sprinkled with a few Italian words.

She opened the door with one hand as she used the other to tuck a dishcloth in her apron.

"So you are my new *bambino*! Come here, Luca!"

Her grasp was strong on my shoulders as she pulled me close for a hug. She smelled of makeup powder and *manjerona*. After a long hug, she grabbed my face with both hands, squeezing my cheeks in her garlicky fingers, then she kissed me twice, the second kiss almost in my eye.

"Let me look at you!" she almost yelled.

Her smile seemed genuine, and my mother smiled with her. Dona Anita's warmth immediately felt like the home we once had.

"And you, my poor soul, you must be Rose. Come here."

My mother walked up to Dona Anita like a child. Dona Anita offered her pale wrinkled hand and my mother enveloped it with hers. Her green eyes stared at my mother's for a moment.

"It's okay," said Mãe.

Dona Anita glanced at the street behinds us, which was already busy with pedestrians, street performers from Peru, and *camelôs* selling novelties smuggled from Paraguay: leather, cassettes, candy, cigarettes, watches, hammocks, and alarm clocks going off one after the other.

"Welcome, welcome! *Vieni*! Let me show you around," she offered.

The front door led to a long poorly lit linoleum corridor, and as we made our way down along its pink walls, I could hear the whistle from a pressure pot growing louder and feel the scent of bean stew taking over.

"I make *feijão* every Monday. Can you smell it?" Her voice echoed through the walkway, as she inhaled intently, as if teaching us how one should smell something.

"The kids are welcome to eat my food. They just need to tell me ahead of time so I'll have enough. I charge four *cruzeiros* per meal. And they can pay me as they go, or I can add it to their rent. *Non importa*." She stopped walking and turned to look at us. Her forehead weaved in a frown. "I don't make profit on food. I like my kids well-fed is all."

"This is great, *filho*," said my mother, nodding several times.

"I have two rooms available now. You'll see them in a second. Let me first show you my kitchen and the dining room."

The kitchen was a small cube overpopulated with pots of different sizes and colors, hanging from hooks on the walls, or tucked under the sink behind a green and white-checkered curtain. The walls were covered in white and yellow tiles. Occasional daisy prints were sprinkled around without any kind of pattern. On the sink there were the different herbs and roots she must have been chopping to season the stew before we interrupted her. A large coffee mug filled with uncooked rice sat next to a green four-burner-stove. On top of the fridge there was a statue of Virgin Mary with a rosary draped over her.

"I cook every day," she said. "But if anything happens, I let everybody know that there won't be a meal."

A little green radio sat on the windowsill at eye level, with its extended antenna reaching the ceiling. Classical music played over the speakers.

"Sometimes they play a little Caruso." She smiled nostalgically.

"That's good," said my mother, although I doubt either of us knew who Enrico Caruso was back then.

"My food is simple. But it keeps them strong. On Fridays, Saturdays, and Sundays I try to make some dessert. Everybody deserves some *dolce* in their lives!" She winked at me.

Dona Anita motioned for us to move into the dining room. There we found a large mahogany table sitting underneath a burnt yellow crystal chandelier, both of which looked so old they could've come from Italy with her, from her great-grandparent's estate.

"Do you miss your home, Dona Anita?" my mother asked, enamored by the crystal chandelier. "Do you miss Italy?"

"This is home!" she barked, rather passionately. "Italy can just eat shit!"

"Oh, *desculpa*, I didn't mean it in that…"

"No, dear. *I* am sorry." Dona Anita got a hold of my mother's hands again. "They should've been nicer to its people, that's all."

Neither of us knew what to say then. I instantly envied the position she was in, the freedom she had to talk about the things that bothered her.

We then took a soapstone stairway up to the second floor, where all the rooms were. Those facing Rua da Praia had more light, she said. But the ones in the back end were more quiet.

"I like quiet."

"Your choice, Luca! But if you like quiet, I believe you should consider the well lit ones by the front, where you can watch the crowd outside. Change things around a bit. See the life. *Capiche?*" She blinked at the both of us this time.

"Sure, why not?" I said, and Dona Anita headed down the hallway, her back turned to us, her head bouncing from side to side as if performing a victory dance.

"Plus if you don't like it, we can always switch. *Facile!* The front rooms are the ones that go quickly."

"How many people do you house here, Dona Anita?" my mother asked as she studied each door we passed by.

"Fifteen boys at full capacity."

"Just boys then?"

"Of course! Can you imagine how they'd behave with *una ragazza* here?" She smiled with an open mouth. "Joking aside, it's not allowed. I would love to have girls here too. I could teach them stuff. How to cook, how to clean. I'm weak, you know. I'm not going to last much longer."

"Don't say that! You're stronger than you think."

"Oh sure. We all are. *Tutti noi!* Anyway, this is it."

She opened the door to room number Eight. Inside was a small single room, with a single lamp on its very center. Its walls were white, and the floors a deep cherry wood parquet. A twin bed had been pushed against the right wall, and a bedside table placed on its left. Underneath the window were a small, narrow desk and a wooden chair, and on the left of it, a little dresser. Dona Anita pushed the window open, then its outer wooden blinds.

"See what I mean?" she asked. Mãe and I squinted at her as our eyes struggled to adapt to such contrast. The morning sun hit us straight in the eye.

"What do you think, *filho*?" my mother was looking at me.

"You don't have to answer now!" Dona Anita interrupted. "Just think about it for a while. And come by again if you need another look."

I looked at Mãe for a moment.

"It's simple. I know. *Troppo umile*. But it's all I can offer." She shrugged her shoulders.

"I want it, Mãe!"

"What about bathrooms?" My mother asked.

"Mãe." I grabbed her shoulders. "This is fine. Better than fine. It's perfect!"

Mãe looked at me.

"Ai, Mãe, don't you worry. *Nona* here will take care of your boy."

Dona Anita finished showing us around, then we all sat down to talk about prices, house rules, lease contract… Since my father had died of lung cancer, a common side effect among miners, my mother was left with a good pension. Enough to not have to worry about getting by, enough to get herself a small place back in Minas do Leão, enough to come to the city every once in a while.

. . .

The bus would drop her off on the side of the road and she had arranged for Mercedes to pick her up. My mother would stay with her friend for, as Mercedes had said, as long as she wished. She would have to find a house. Small – for herself only. In her head she pictured something simple with as much white as possible, and tile floors. A small backyard would be good too. Then she would have to find somebody to move whatever she had saved in storage back to Minas do Leão. A couple pieces of furniture, her kitchen utensils, her gardening tools and almost all of Pablo's belongings.

Aside from the smell, the bus was fairly comfortable but the road so awful she thought she would get sick and make a fool of herself. She watched as her surroundings gradually became more and more rural, the businesses more sparse. She had thought she would find comfort in the meadow, on watching the animals aimlessly waste their days, on tending to her vegetable garden, on reuniting with old friends. She thought the simpler life was what she wanted. What she needed.

When the doctor told her my father would probably not survive that winter, she had secretly begun to look forward to the move. It was my last year of college, and she was just tired. But as Mãe noticed the outskirts of Porto Alegre disappear behind her, she wondered for the very first time, if maybe she'd be too lonely, lost in an even more remote past.

"This is it, *senhora*," announced the bus driver as he pulled over. The brakes screeching until the bus finally came to a stop.

The other passengers looked around, out the window, and at each other, trying to guess what that obscure town would be. My mother got up from her seat, and headed for the front door, looking straight ahead.

"Is someone coming for you, *senhora*?"

"*Sim*, my friend should be here soon," she said as she held onto the driver's calloused hand and made her way down the steps. "*Obrigada*."

The afternoon sun dappled the road ahead of them with little puddles of light. The air smelled of sulfur and mud and fire and manure and home. But what was it? How would it ever be home? What was home but a memory?

She hadn't seen that much green in a long time. It was strange to suddenly realize the vastness of Minas do Leão, this tiny town, compared to how packed and claustrophobic Porto Alegre could be. Her world was suddenly big again, and she wasn't sure that was a good thing.

The air was crisp, as the *minuano* blew steady, but the meadow already showed signs of the coming spring. My mother buttoned up her cardigan and folded her arms across her chest. Mercedes was nowhere in sight. The bus driver carefully placed her six bags on the side of the road, then looked around. The meadow stretching for miles. A few *quero-queros* were flying by, but for miles they were the only people out.

"*Muito obrigada, senhor*," said Mãe.

"No need." He stared at the deserted road with her. "I can wait a couple minutes until your friend gets here."

They both waited. Then the driver asked what time her friend was supposed to be there. My mother's gaze was frozen, lost somewhere in all that land. She shifted her shoulders.

"I don't know," she said, almost like a whisper.

"You don't know?" The driver couldn't disguise his astonishment.

"What?"

"Did you tell your friend what time…?"

"*Ah, sim*. Of course. She will be here a little before five."

"Alright. Soon then. I'll stay a couple minutes."

"Don't worry. I'll be fine on my own." She looked at her six bags. "But thank you."

The driver ignored her words and stood next to her. His hands in his pockets. As time went by, the other passengers were getting up from their seats and peeking out the window as they tried to understand what the hold up was. Sensing their anxiety, my mother looked behind her, and saw a few trying to pry open their heavy windows, a man making his way down to the steps.

"You should go," she said, nodding sideways to show what was happening with the other passengers.

The driver apologized to my mother several times, making his way back into the bus.

"Have a safe trip!" she offered.

He tipped his cap by the door. His eyes locked with hers for about two seconds. The second time that week this had happened to her. A stranger looking her in the eye, as if she were a real person, whole, and she wondered if she could behave like one.

Mãe saw the bus pick up speed as it continued down the road, eventually disappearing on a right curve. Everything but her thoughts was quiet. She circled her belongings trying to find a spot she was comfortable standing by, to no avail.

The blue and orange and purple and pink across the sky were all familiar to her. She had many times dreamt of going back, of watching the colors shift as the sun set beyond the coal mine, and its black infinite landscape. But she had never seen it from that perspective, never from the side of the road, from the outskirts of town. Never as a widow.

And from that deserted road, each shift of colors in the sky, each inch the sun lowered itself, each bird that glided through the horizon or dog that crossed that road as if it had somewhere to be, was yet another unnatural event she had to witness and endure. Several little incidents, and numerous major catastrophes, shattering the idea one had of one's own self, forcing her to live with parts of her she didn't recognize. Like little tragedy trinkets.

. . .

"We'll have fettuccini tonight if you'd like to eat with us. It would be good to meet some of the other boys." Dona Anita yelled over some orchestra playing on her radio.

She sat at her kitchen table cutting up strings of dough with a steak knife. There was flour everywhere on and around her. Dona Anita sprinkled flour over some cut up pieces, picking them up and carefully and quickly placing them on a plastic bowl.

"That would be great. Count me in!" I finished my glass of water, washed it and placed it back on the counter. "Thank you."

"*Prego*, my dear!" She smiled tenderly, over more flat dough. "You'll like my fettuccini. Everyone likes my fettuccini! Since it's your first night I'll go ahead and make some dessert too. Do you like *pavê de chocolate*? It's my specialty!"

"I love it! Thanks! That's very kind!"

"Oh Luca, stop it! There's no need to be that formal here! *Dio mio*! This is your home now!"

I said okay and gave her an awkward smile, but the last time I had been around an elder person was back home, and my father would have been livid with me if he saw that I wasn't using ma'am and sir, and whatever else was proper. I excused myself and headed up to my room. From the stairs I heard Dona Anita yelling, "Fettuccini and *pavê* tonight!" And immediately after I heard an equally loud "Yes! I love you, Nona!"

That evening as we gathered around the dining table, Dona Anita introduced me to each of the other students.

"Hey man, I'm Francisco. From Bento Gonçalves. Studying Engineering at PUC."

And there was Fernando, first semester at UFRGS, from Bagé; Paulo, third semester, PUC, from Caxias do Sul.

Soon enough, I was Luca, last semester at UFRGS. Literature. From Minas do Leão.

"Where is that?" asked Paulo. Paulo was a short, long-haired hippie. He wore brown corduroy pants and a shirt that read *"Coração de Estudante,"* a Milton Nascimento song that almost instantly had become an anthem nationwide for the student movement against the dictatorship.

"It's actually fairly close to here. About two hour drive at most. A mining town. At least it used to be. Close to Arroio dos Ratos."

"I wouldn't know where that is either."

"Can someone help me get the plates?" Dona Anita yelled from the kitchen. And I was relieved to leave.

"Not you, boy. This is your first night. Go talk to people. Let the others do the work. You'll have plenty of chances to help." I stood there watching her, waiting for her to change her mind. *"Andiamo!"* she yelled.

When we sat down there were about seven of us plus Dona Anita at the very end of the table. She was right, her pasta was delicious, probably the best I had my whole life.

Francisco from Bento Gonçalves was the most talkative of all. But Fernando from Bagé was so quiet it was disturbing. He was the youngest too.

"I go to UFRGS too. What are you studying?" I asked him.

"Business," he said without looking up.

"Do you like it?"

"I don't care. I had to leave the farm. It's just something to do." His eyes were fixed on his plate, even though he was done eating.

"Oh."

I glanced at Dona Anita and by her frown I could tell we were in dangerous territory. I was ready to drop the subject.

"They took my father. This fucking regime."

"Language, Fernando!" Dona Anita shrieked, her mouth full of pasta.

"I'm sorry," he whispered absent-mindedly. "There's just no point." Something about his tone hit me the wrong way, as if he was the only one going through this.

"I lost my brother too."

"Sorry. Losing your father is tough though."

"My father died last week." I could feel my blood rushing up to my cheeks. "My brother was younger than I am today when he disappeared. There's a lot he never got a chance to do."

Fernando eyed me for two seconds. Rage spilling out of his eyeballs.

"I'm just saying." I shrugged, but he kept on staring at me.

"Well, how about some *pavê*?" Dona Anita slapped the table with both hands.

She watched us all devour it in silence. Her arms crossed. A satisfied smile on her face.

I looked at her and she must've guessed what I was thinking.

"I don't eat it anymore. I've had it all my life. And it's a long one as you can tell."

As I was walking up the stairs to my room, Francisco came up to me. "Don't worry," he whispered. "My first dinner here was just as awkward. If not worse. Tomorrow will be better."

"Hey boys," Dona Anita called. "Ronaldo just called from the public market. They'll have beans tomorrow. Can anybody get in line?"

"I can go this time," Francisco yelled.

"Grazie, Chico! I'll have the money for you tomorrow."

"What is this line she's talking about?" I asked him.

"Food line," he said very matter-of-factly, and I frowned. "What, you never heard of a food line? What country do you live in?"

"Is it cheaper this way? Through this line I mean?"

"No! It's the only way! Ever since the coup."

I was baffled. Mãe had never mentioned such a thing, let alone ask us to get in line for her.

"Do you usually eat meals here?"

"Eh," he shrugged, brushed his hair back with his fingers. "Dinners more often. Let me know if you ever need anything."

Francisco was in room Five.

. . .

Seven hundred and one. He had spent his morning recounting every little mark he had made on the walls. Every little line he had scraped was a day he had spent in that cell. Each day he questioned his own memory all over again and recounted every single one of them. Each day he considered blocking them off and writing out the number to prevent having to recount them. Maybe by the hundreds. But, then, what would he do all day?

Seven hundred and one days without a trial. Without news from his family. The only news Pablo ever got were the deaths of some of his *companheiros*. X was taken to the river; no teeth left in his mouth. Y didn't survive the electric shocks; smoke blew out of his hair. Z had a heart attack when the guards made him watch his wife being raped. Someone said he was ready to say everything he knew, that he was about to give them all they could possibly want from him. It wouldn't have made a difference. He would have died anyway.

Seven hundred and one days and he couldn't think of why they would ever let him out, why they would let him live. And this wasn't the only cell he'd been in. He thought he had spent over a hundred days at the Ilha do Presídio, but who could tell at this point? He shouldn't trust his own memory.

He sat on the cement floor with his back against the wall reminding himself of all the things which made him who he was, all the things he couldn't say in that place.

I am Pablo Fonte. Born on November 6th, 1949. My mother is Rose. My little brother is Luca, born on September 1st 1953. My father was a miner. Antonio. We live on Rua do Arvoredo, number... number? How could he have forgotten this? He looked at his thin veiny arms hanging from his boney shoulders, as his hands rested on the dirty floor. Black underneath his nails. *What is our street number?*

"It doesn't matter," he said. Out loud this time.

Rita was my only girlfriend. She lives on...

"Oh for Christ's sake!" Quick, short breaths.

He looked at the small opening on the door from which the guards would every once in a while monitor him. Fluorescent white spilled in from the grid. The only source of light he had. He crawled across the floor, and sat next to the door, his legs curled up under his chin. He could feel the floor pulsating as someone walked by. He lifted his hand and watched the path his veins created within his hands and arms.

We live on Rua do Arvoredo, number...

Tears streamed down his face, and he tried to lick them with his tongue because he was thirsty, and because that had to be better than drinking from the toilet bowl.

Without hesitation, Pablo sunk his teeth into his wrist as deep as he could. His breathing accelerating from the pain and adrenaline. Tears and blood trickled down his arm and legs, his jaw cramped like a wild animal. He struggled to be as quiet as he possibly could, never letting go. But his blood tasted bitter, and he could feel his empty stomach turning as he swallowed some of it. If he got sick that would be the end. He would fail. Again. A small crimson puddle was forming to his right. He heard himself panting.

"*Ajuda! Ajuda aqui!*" It sounded like an echo at the very end of a tunnel.

Pablo shut his eyes, letting go of his arm. His head hung from his neck as if his neck was made of rubber.

"*Não, companheiro!* You can't do this! It's what they want you to do!"

He felt dizzy. Nauseous. He could feel several hands around him, touching him, moving his body this way and that. Someone wrapped something cottony around his wrist and held his arm up to the ceiling.

Another caressed his long hair, repeating over and over that it was okay, that everything would be okay. Someone whispered Hail Mary in his ear as he held on to Pablo like you would a child. Both bodies rocking back and forth.

"Shh, shh, shh, shh, shh."

ELEVEN

HE SAT ON a bench at a bus stop on the corner of Borges and Salgado Filho. While the sun slowly disappeared behind the port warehouses, he waited, watching one bus after another approach their final stop and unload dozens of exhausted passengers. His beard was long and itchy, but too sparse. His head was shaved, exposing the crescent moon scar he carried with him from the time he had slipped inside the mine, falling headfirst on a rock. He was four when it had happened, and our father had carried him in his arms, across the wet meadow all the way to our house. Pablo's head bouncing with each step. Blood soaking and staining our father's right sleeve. Now Pablo covered the scar with a cap because that too could be telling.

He was living at Chico's house, along with other *clandestinos*. Of course that wasn't his real name. None of them used their real names. Chico knew a couple of doctors they could trust and those who could afford them would go for a new nose, a new smile, a new hairline. Chico also had papers now. He had officially become Francisco dos Santos. But there was a cost. And most of his housemates would do the same things as Pablo: a haircut, a beard, bake their skin in the sun or avoid it like the devil, lose or gain weight, whichever they could do more of.

Pablo's appetite hadn't been the same after prison. He would get severe stomach pains whenever he ate something heavier. *Churrasco* wasn't even worth the trouble anymore. When he'd manage to find the image of a pink undercooked steak appetizing, when he'd find a way to block the images of exposed flesh from his mind, his stomach would still act up, and he would almost immediately have to curl himself into a ball with severe cramps.

On his first week out he had walked back to Rua do Arvoredo to see our house. He had sat across the street from it, and what he found was an older couple, who spent their afternoons sitting on the porch. The man would doze and wake up to a car door being shut, a bus speeding up, or a dog barking at a delivery boy on his bicycle. The woman never slept. She would occasionally pick up her yarn and knit for a minute or two, then stop again, glance at her snoozing husband, and her eyes would shift back to the street.

Pablo had been at Chico's for about two months when he asked my brother to go meet somebody at a bus stop and lead him back to his place. My brother had sat on that same bench he was on now. Whoever he was supposed to meet, green sweater, was late. It was cold then and he had pulled his scarf up to his nose, covering most of his face, and wore the same cap, always refraining from making eye contact with anybody. Except when he saw what looked to be his old shoes on somebody else's feet stepping out of the bus, one of the last people to get out, and although afraid to look up to the person's face, afraid of being recognized without having thought it through before, he still did, he still looked into that young man's eyes, and what he found was not his little brother, not the little boy who was constantly showing up in his dreams, constantly looking up to him, searching for answers, always available to go anywhere he would take him. No. It wasn't him. What he found was a young man, an adult, dressed in work clothes, walking as though he owed nothing to nobody, as though he was his own person. Pablo froze as soon as he realized what was happening, and looked out of the corner of his eye as I made my way down Salgado Filho, then disappeared from his view when I turned right on Borges.

Pablo went back to the same bus stop several times after that. Always at rush hour.

...

Rita and I would bump into each other sometimes at random places and we kept in touch that way. One evening though, I was in my room writing when Dona Anita knocked on my door.

"There's a lady on the phone wanting to speak to you," she said, stretching the word 'lady' as wide as her suggestive smile.

It was Rita saying she had found the number in the yellow pages, asking if she could come over, if they allowed girls in the rooms. Dona Anita said it was fine as long as she showed her her ID.

"*Ah, legal!* Okay, I'll see you in thirty minutes. Is that okay with you?"

"Perfect!" I said.

"Okay, *beijo.*"

I hung up and headed upstairs to clean my room and take a shower. Francisco saw my bedroom door open and walked over, his hands in his pockets, a grin I recognized.

"Dona Anita said you're bringing a girl over!" He leaned against the doorframe. "Didn't know you had a girl, *seu come quieto.*"

"Knock it off, man. She's just a friend."

But the truth is I couldn't contain my smile. I loved being around her. She was the only person in this town who knew me before all this, and she was beautiful in such way that when you looked at her, you believed there was a god.

"Are you guys going out somewhere?"

"No, I guess we're just staying here," I shrugged.

"Hey, do you want to borrow my radio? There's an all Beatles show tonight at 102.3. You're welcome to it, if you want."

"Sure."

By the time I was plugging it in, Dona Anita yelled from downstairs. Rita had arrived, and I ran down to meet her. She wore a canary yellow tank top tucked into her faded bellbottom denim. Her hair was loose, and draped over the large backpack she carried on her.

"Now you two behave yourselves, okay?" Dona Anita warned us as we made our way upstairs. "*Buonanotte!*"

"I brought wine," Rita whispered. "I don't think it's any good, but there's a lot of it."

When we got to my room, she showed me what she had meant. Rita had stopped at the public market on her way over and bought a gallon of wine, like the bottles my mother kept at home to make *quentão* with, along with a small colonial cheese and a quarter kilo of bread.

"Whoa, fantastic!"

"It's nothing!" She smiled. "How are you?" She looked me in the eye. "This is great! I love this place!" She scanned the room, then looked out the window. "Can't believe you have a window facing Rua da Praia! This is my dream! You get to see everything that happens. Really, who needs a television with a window like yours?! This is so perfect!"

I took a seat on the floor, with my back against the bed, as she studied everything with the curiosity of a child. She knocked on the dresser as if to test the wood it was made of, she pulled up the desk chair, sat down facing the window.

"Luca, I'm so jealous! This is the best place to study!" She rested her arms on the table, looked out again. "Just perfect! Oh, I don't have glasses though. Or a knife," she said, still watching the few pedestrians down the street. "I mean, we could just drink it out of the bottle. It's fine by me."

"I'll get some. I'll be right back." I ran downstairs then back up, afraid she'd be gone if I left her by herself for too long.

"You didn't tell me how you were doing," she said as soon as I walked in.

She had opened the bottle of wine and unwrapped the bread.

"I'm great! It's good to see you! It's weird having you here."

I poured her some wine.

"I know. That's good," she said taking her glass from me. "I like it here though!"

"I do, too. *Tim tim?*"

We toasted, and Rita made a face after her first sip.

"It will taste better by the second glass!" She laughed, her lips tinged purple until she licked them.

"Do you want some music?"

She nodded, and I turned the radio on. Francisco had already set the radio station, and the chorus of *I Want to Hold Your Hand* blasted through it. I turned the volume way down.

"Did you see their movie yet? Every once in a while they show it again at the theater down the street," she said, pointing to the left as she took a seat on the desk chair. "It's so good!"

"A couple times. *Sim.*"

She downed her glass. Her wavy hair came down to her waist as she tilted her head back, waiting for the last drops of wine to slip into her mouth.

"How about some cheese? The bread was still warm when I picked it up!" She arched her brows into question marks. I poured us more wine.

"So what's up, Rita?" By the look in her eyes, I could tell she knew exactly what I meant.

She drank some more, turned to the window. The street was gradually quieting down.

"I heard there's supposed to be a procession tonight. A group of women will be walking through this street. It's the birth of a new movement. They want amnesty. They want their children, their husbands back."

She sat on the desk, watching the street again. I waited. Drank some more. She looked down to the parquet floor, as if embarrassed.

"What's wrong?" I asked.

She was playing with her hair, curling it around her finger.

"I should've told you before coming here. I thought it would be fun to get drunk. But I also wanted to see what these women are doing. I thought you would've talked me out of it." Her green eyes were moist.

"Rita, it's fine! It's really fine! You were right, this is fun. Let's have fun then! Don't cry, *por favor!*"

"I'm sorry, Luca." She patted underneath her eyes, trying

not to mess her makeup.

"Just forget it. No reason to feel sorry. But…" I paused. "You were right. I would've tried to talk you out of it. You gotta move on. It's been too long."

The words coming out of my mouth tasted like cheap plastic. I wanted to hug her, but I was afraid of what she would think of it. Afraid of what she would think of me.

"Oh c'mon, Luca!" she barked.

I looked at her, surprised by her tone.

"Did *you* stop?" she asked with an accusatory look, as she munched on a piece of bread.

"What do you mean?"

"I see the writing all over town that's what I mean!" Rita's eyes drifted back to the window again.

The fact was that I had stopped following rebels around ever since that incident with the marbles. Clearly I wasn't meant to be among them. I would, though, sometimes go to the places I had already been and rewrite the message. I would still write Pablo's words at public parks, bus stations…But I wanted nothing to do with those people ever since that night. I liked being on my own. I was comfortable that way.

Rita was staring at me.

"Look, all I'm saying is sometimes it feels good to do something, to be part of something that might lead to change. It's good for me. It's good for you. That's why we both do this."

I never thought anything I did would lead to change. Just didn't think of it that way.

"Fair enough," I said. "What time are these women walking?"

She shrugged. "I think around ten. We have some time. *Queijo?*" She smiled again. Rita could smile with her eyes too.

By ten o'clock we were both pretty drunk. Rita had talked nonstop about the boys she'd been with, the day Clara and I had caught her and Pablo kissing for the first time, about the time she got to see the ocean and how good it smelled, and how her toes had hurt so much from the freezing water. She talked about her dreams of going to Rio, and Liverpool, and Rome. About saying goodbye to this city, this fucking country. She talked and I listened. We had switched the light off and were sitting on my desk waiting for these women to show up. Hardly anybody on the street. Rita occasionally looked at me to make sure I was still with her. Her eyes shone from the night-light and all the alcohol. Had I ever managed to win her love or whatever she had felt for my brother, I wouldn't have given it up for anything in this world.

"How about you?" she whispered. "Don't you have a story?"

I looked out the window trying to think of something worthy. She had so much life in her, that I wished that she would talk for days.

"You know, for a while, I thought it was him. Writing," she said staring at her almost empty glass.

"Oh."

"I would think that he was hiding somewhere. But still here."

I was such a jerk for doing this to her. Rita sipped her wine.

"How did you figure it out?" I asked.

"You, telling me, just now."

"What?"

"I mean, the handwriting was different of course, and at some random places too. Plus the fact that none of us had news from him."

I could feel a pang of guilt building up right in my stomach.

"The truth is wishful thinking is a powerful thing, and it could have been any of his friends. Anybody really. But I so wanted it to be him."

"I don't know what to say, Rita. I'm very sorry."

"Really, it's fine. It makes sense actually. And I can't pretend like I'm the only one going through this, right?"

I stuck my head out the window and looked up as grayish clouds were expanding and drifting across the black blue sky. When I looked back down, I noticed the group of women approaching our block.

"Rita! They're here!" I whispered.

"*Ai meu Deus!*" she whispered back. We both sipped more wine.

There must have been around thirty or forty women, all dressed in black, each holding a white candle. They formed a solid block, as if their bodies together created something greater and unique. An entity of sorts. Some kind of spiritual identity. They walked very slowly, as if afraid to disturb the air around them. They didn't chant anything, they didn't pray, not aloud anyway, they didn't talk to each other. They just walked in pairs, holding on to their candle with one hand, and their partners with the other.

Rita held on to her glass with both hands. Her fingers wrapped around it as she brought it close to her face and took a deep breath.

Once the women were close enough I noticed that none of them cried, none of them showed anger, despair, none of their faces seemed to fight their predicament. And yet that was exactly what they were doing. They were fighting. Rita was right. This was a different kind of protest.

I looked at other windows across the street and didn't see anybody else watching them. I looked back at the group trying to guess who these mothers and wives could possibly be. One woman at the very back looked up at us, as if she wanted us to notice her, as if she was trying to engrave her face in our memories should anything happen to them, to her. I nodded and she nodded back, her partner looked straight ahead, oblivious to our quick exchange. I wondered if that woman could have sensed our presence, our eyes on her, if that was what had made her look up to our window. Or if she had been seeking a witness the whole time, longingly searching someone to see her, someone to give her the courage she needed to keep going despite her fears.

"I should've been with them." Rita whispered. Her chin quivering as a tear slipped down her left cheek.

Rita tilted her empty glass in my direction and I poured us both more wine. We waited quietly as the women kept going.

"I hate this city," she said eventually, looking at their backs then, and I nodded.

"*Sim*," I agreed.

"It's nothing but a fucking sunset."

"Very true."

"I hate this fucking country." She brought her glass to her lips.

"Me too."

"I just hate being stuck here."

I touched her hand and she grabbed mine, like a baby would do. Instinctively. The women continued to walk very slowly, barely making progress. When I looked at Rita, I saw her eyes fixed to these women's backs, as if part of her walked with them. The part that would never be available to me.

. . .

My mother had always been intrigued by Joào's death. Back when Mercedes called her to let her know, she had just said, "He's gone, Rose. Just gone." When she moved back to Minas do Leào, she had asked again what had happened, and if it had anything to do with his lungs, like my father, but Mercedes had dismissed her, "I don't know what got hold of him. Doesn't matter now. He's dead." A bitterness in her voice my mother not only recognized, but could also taste it in her own mouth as sharp as if biting into a fresh cut lime.

My mother had since stopped asking.

Little Junior was seven years old and blond as a *polaco*. He couldn't even walk outside without turning pink-red like a shrimp. He was a good boy though. If it was up to him, he would waste his days around his mother, like a fruit fly, enamored by her sweet, nourishing scent, always asking questions, offering help, always watching her, and what he didn't realize was that sometimes she just wanted to be left alone. My mother would watch out for these moments, when Mercedes would just stare past the boy's shoulders when he talked to her, her eyes crinkled at the corners as he whined to get her attention, or when she would stand by the kitchen sink, the water running wastefully, her gaze somewhere deep in the creases of her bungalow's wood planks. My mother would convince little Junior to help her weed the backyard, climb up the guava tree so they could make jam that evening, or maybe go check if Mr. Mancuso at the corner *armazém* had any fresh spicy sausage for an *arroz com linguiça* for dinner. Whatever she could do to give her friend a break.

December was only a couple days away, and my mother was already having trouble falling asleep, already struggling to push her thoughts back into the little caves inside her brain where they wouldn't bother her. The brain, she thought, was much like the coal mine. From the surface one would never guess what went on underground; its maze, its dead-ended routes, its deep dark inner workings. Slippery, and filled with traps that could send you on a journey with no return. She much preferred the flat, bright surface with its mud and gravel and grass, sprinkled with occasional *azedinhas*, over the richness and murky sophistication of down below. But December had become the month of dwelling within these caves. She knew that and couldn't help it, however hard she tried. It would be six years without news.

"I was thinking of staying until the end of January," my mother said. "Would that be okay with you?"

The two of them sat in the dark kitchen, sipping chamomile tea, listening to the sound of night crickets and sleepless frogs. Little Junior had been asleep for hours. The lantern outside of Mercedes's bungalow would seep through her kitchen window, making it just clear enough to see everything, without feeling too exposed in their nightgowns. They certainly were good friends. But this level of intimacy didn't come easy for either one of them.

"He killed himself," Mercedes said, staring out the window.

My mother looked up from her tea. Inhaled deeply.

"Killed himself," she repeated. "They found him in the meadow, halfway between your house and the mine."

"*Meu Deus*, Mercedes. I didn't know. I am very sorry." My mother could feel her eyes overflowing.

"Hanged himself from a tree branch. Not far from the creek." She was playing with the spoon in her teacup.

"Dear God," my mother whispered. In a fraction of a second, she remembered the sight of her friend's bare feet inside that creek what seemed like a life ago, as everybody danced and chanted hymns around her.

"Tree wasn't even tall enough," she said. "He knelt down to die."

Mercedess brought her hands to her face, breaking into spasms, hiccups; her eyes completely dry.

"Oh my friend, my dear friend, my poor thing." My mother held her hand.

"I mean, how much do you have to want to die?" Her eyes were blood red. "The whole time he could've just gotten up, he could've thought of us. He could have thought of his son he wanted so much, and not been a selfish bastard." She paused to look at my mother, as if to make sure her words were not repulsive to her. "How could he do this after all we went through to build a family?"

"Does Junior know?"

She shook her head. "But everyone does. He'll find out soon enough."

My mother couldn't sleep that night. She had sat at the edge of Mercedes' bed, caressing her friend's hair. Across the horizon, she could see a hint of purple as dawn approached. She opened the living room window, allowing the cool morning breeze to come in and bring with it the smell of wet earth she had missed almost as much as she missed her old self. A thick palpable fog and a light drizzle settled over the deep green meadow, like a bride's veil.

Right before drifting to a deep sleep, Mercedes had asked, pleaded actually, for my mother to stay with them. They could cut costs that way, they could keep each other company, and little Junior clearly seemed happier ever since my mother's arrival, she'd said. At first it sounded absurd to her. My mother wanted her own house. She had gotten used to the idea of growing old alone. She wasn't afraid. But as she watched the sun appear in the thin slit between the horizon and the heavy clouds, she pictured a row of red roses across the front fence, she measured with her eyes if the backyard could accommodate another room they could attach to the back of the house. She walked out the front door, made her way to the dirt road outside and took a long look at her friend's pastel pink house. It wasn't tall like she had imagined, she wouldn't watch the sun set beyond the mine from her kitchen window. But she liked how imposing and self-sufficient Mercedes' guava and avocado trees seemed in her front yard, like two big buffers. A steady gray rain was falling on her shoulders now, and she thought about going inside, about trying to get some sleep. But this was the rain she had been waiting for. My mother stood there, and let it soak her as she studied her new home.

. . .

I was reading in my room one evening when I heard someone banging on the front door downstairs. Francisco's radio down the hall played some progressive music I didn't recognize. I stuck my head out the window and saw three officers standing outside, one of them using his baton against Dona Anita's door.

"*Buona sera, signori.* What brings you here at this hour?" She sounded as though she was standing next to me.

"Good evening, ma'am. We're very sorry to bother you this late." Dona Anita let out a loud yawn as the men talked. "But we were informed that there's a terrorist living in your pension."

"A what?" Dona Anita yelled in shock.

"A terrorist, ma'am. We're looking for someone known as Padre."

"You must be in the wrong place. I have no *ragazzo* named Padre, and I have no priests here either."

"Unfortunately, ma'am, sometimes these people use a different militant identity as their own."

I went down to Francisco's room and told him what was going on.

"What was the name?" he asked.

"They said Padre."

"Shit." He was quiet for a moment. "Everyone's gotta know."

"Okay."

"But quietly," he added, then headed down the corridor.

Dona Anita was making her way upstairs.

"Where is Carlos?" she asked in a whisper I didn't realize she was capable of.

"In his room. I think Francisco may be in there."

"Gather everybody to go downstairs. I'll go talk to Carlos," she said and headed down the hallway to his room.

"Luca," Dona Anita whispered yet again. "Don't go downstairs without me. Wait for me here, *capisce*?"

I nodded.

When Dona Anita met us in the hallway, we were all lined up, leaning against the wall.

"Everybody ready?"

"Where is Carlos?" Fernando asked.

"He's not here," said Dona Anita.

"But I..."

"Fernando! Carlos is not here!" A harsh whisper.

We made our way down the steps. I turned to Francisco, and he gave me a 'I'll explain later' look.

"Here they are. I'm sorry I took so long, I had to wake some of them up." Dona Anita said in a tone that sounded more like hers, but not quite.

The officers stood by the front door, carefully studying each one of us, whispering amongst themselves, then looking back at us again. Some of us would yawn, or lean back against the wall, close our eyes, pretend exhaustion, boredom, indifference. I looked at Francisco again, and he just forced another yawn like the others.

"I told you, no *terroristas* in my house. They are all good students."

The officers asked each of us to give them our full names. One after another, we gave them what they wanted. They would make us repeat ourselves, or have further questions, or just ask something about Padre.

When I told them my name, the one officer who had been quiet all along squinted his eyes at me.

"What did you say?"

"Luca Fonte. My name is Luca Fonte."

"Fonte?" He tucked his hands inside his pockets, lifted his chin up, and looked down at me.

"Yes, sir." I said.

"Uhuh."

They continued on down the line. When they were done, one of the officers pursed his lips, making it almost disappear underneath his untamed mustache, then nodded to Dona Anita.

"Listen, ma'am. We're gonna need to search the rooms. Make sure nobody is hiding anybody. Okay?"

Dona Anita frowned.

"And we'll need each man to stand by their door, so we know what belongs to whom. Do you understand?" he asked her, and I could tell by the look in her eyes that she was fuming inside, that all she wanted was to give him a good smack. "It's not that we don't trust you, ma'am. It's our job. *Lavoro.*"

"I know what 'job' is, child! Why don't you stick to yours then and stop trying to be cute here? I don't need no translator," said Dona Anita. Francisco struggled to swallow his laughter. "You can do your search. Stay as long as you need. But don't you go messing up my house, or I'll call the police on you," she warned him.

The three men looked everywhere, her kitchen, the dinning room, inside cabinets, in every bedroom… By then we all had already heard different stories of how the military behaved when they searched people's homes, how sometimes they were no different than burglars or other criminals, how sometimes they were much worse.

Dona Anita trailed behind them like a boss, not at all intimidated. I, on the other hand, couldn't seem to make my calves stop shaking. I had no guns, no names, no lists. But what if they found the marbles? The spray paint?

When they finished looking upstairs they turned to her.

"Where are the other two?"

"*Scusi?*"

"The other two students, ma'am. There are fourteen occupied rooms. Only twelve boys." The mustached one had a triumphant look in his eyes as if he had just discovered a hole in Einstein's theory of relativity.

"Oh. One works as a night watchman at a residential building in Menino Deus. I don't have the address though, or else I'd give it to you. I can ask him next time he is home. The other had to leave town about three weeks ago. His *babbo* had a stroke and he had to tend to him and their farm. Not sure when he'll be back."

"What are their names?"

"Carlos and Roberto."

"Which is which?" he asked impatiently.

"Roberto is the night watchman. Carlos is with his *babbo.*"

The three of them scanned our faces for a moment.

"Can I help you with anything else?" Dona Anita asked.

"No, ma'am. We're gonna go now. I'm…"

"I'll walk you out," she interrupted. "Boys, you may go back to bed now," she announced loudly, and we dispersed as Dona Anita and the three of them made their way down the stairs.

From my window, I saw them walk out the front door and take a seat at the corner *boteco.*

Later that evening, Francisco knocked on my door.

"Still awake?" he whispered.

"Come in," I said.

He walked in, opened the window to let enough light inside, lit up a cigarette and sat on the floor, his back against the wall.

"What the hell just happened?" I asked with a nervous laugh. "Is Dona Anita...?"

"Dona Anita has nothing to do with anything. Relax!"

He took a drag then offered it to me. I shook my head.

"She knows who is, though. She knows who is involved. She knows the names they use. And she will help them if the DOPS ever comes here, like tonight. That's all there is to it."

"Oh." I sat up on my bed. "I'll take that cigarette."

Francisco handed it to me.

"And where is Carlos?"

"She hid him. There's some kind of false floor here. I heard it leads to the neighbor's basement or something. She won't tell us, and whoever has been there can't say a word."

"Do you know who is involved?" I asked, handing him his cigarette back. The smoke felt smooth in my throat.

"I only know two. Carlos and another one. And I only know this because a similar thing happened about five months ago."

"Hmm." I stuck my hand out and he passed me his cigarette.

"I knew Carlos was, though. A couple months ago he gave me some stuff to hide in my room."

"And Padre?" I asked, rather astonished.

Francisco laughed.

"What?"

"Apparently his family wanted him to become a priest. He ran away from seminary after three months. Straight to a whorehouse." He laughed.

TWELVE

MY MOTHER INSISTED on coming down to Porto Alegre on the day I would receive my diploma from one of the dean's assistants. I had decided that participating in the ceremony would be a waste of money, but she still wanted to watch the person hand me the document, as if it were some kind of blessing.

I waited for her at the bus station. Mãe was one of the first people out, her eyes scanned the crowds.

"Mãe!" I yelled and waved to her from behind the iron fence that separated us. Cigarette smoke formed a cloud above all of us waiting for passengers' arrival.

My mother gave out a wide smile and followed my voice, looking much younger than I remembered. She had curled her hair, and done her make-up, a rosy lipstick glistened as she talked as if we were the only ones there, as if all were quiet and we could hear each other, as if we were standing side by side. She quickly made her way through the crowd, straightening the wrinkles of her daisy printed dress. Her white shawl trailing behind her.

"*Meu filho!*" I heard her say, still a couple meters away.

"*Oi* Mãe!"

"*Meu filho*, wow, you've really come into your own!" she sighed.

I hugged her. She smelled of roses like always.

"A few months away from me, and you look so much older. Like a man."

"And you like a little girl."

She blushed.

"Don't be silly. Your mother here is getting old."

We were walking out of the bus station, away from the crowds.

"I can tell Minas do Leão is treating you well!"

"I like working the land. I like its vastness. And little Junior keeps me busy." Her face lit up when she talked about Mercedes' boy. "He gets mad at me when I call him Luca though." She smiled.

Outside was a gray thick heat.

"Could you please take us to UFRGS?" I asked the cab driver at the front of the line, and motioned for Mãe to get in.

"It's still early. But I thought we could grab a coffee or something. I could show you around campus. You've never been there, have you?"

She shook her head. "That sounds lovely, *filho*."

Campus was almost deserted. None of the cliques were smoking around the ashtray on the plaza, nobody ran late to class, no couples sat under a tree to kiss each other as if no one was watching.

Mãe picked up that day's Zero Hora as we waited to be called at the dean's office.

"How come you never asked me or Pablo to get in line for you?" I asked.

"What? What are you talking about?"

"Food line. At Dona Anita's we rotate. How come you never told us? Did Pai know? Did he get in line for you?"

"He knew. But he never got in line." She looked up at the blooming *jacarandá* tree outside the window. "I don't know why, honestly. I guess I thought you had been asked enough, guess I figured you two had to deal with enough changes. I don't know."

"But I could've helped, especially after Pai's illness. I just never pictured you in those lines, just always figured there was another way."

"Don't! I think I actually liked getting out of the house. Maybe that's why I never said anything."

My mother was disappointed with the way the woman handed me my diploma, like it didn't mean anything, but we still had a nice afternoon. I took her out to a *churrascaria* down on Avenida Farrapos and we ate until we couldn't stand the smell of barbecue any longer, and then we walked along the empty streets as we waited for the late bus, which would take her back home.

"So you're not coming anytime soon, are you?" she asked when we sat on a bench across from the cathedral.

"I don't know, Mãe. I'll visit you. There's just a lot going on right now. Maybe I'll come down in February for a couple of days. I hate *carnaval* anyway."

"Okay, *filho*." She looked at her own shoes. "You got your own life and I understand that and am happy for you. I only invite you because I think you might like it there. You could teach at the local school." She smiled, embarrassed.

I looked up as the bell tolled 8pm.

"Well, I'm sure handsome as you are there's a line of girls following you around, and you are probably just now taking advantage of being in a large city like this."

I smiled and thought of Rita and how confused she made me feel, how I wished that I could pursue her, that she would pursue me, that she would want that, and how awful I felt for even considering such nonsense.

"Have you seen Rita lately?"

Her question really startled me. "Not really." I lied. "We bump into each other every once in a while around the neighborhood."

She nodded. "Her mother wants to move back, too. I think she might, eventually."

"That would be good for you."

"Eh. I don't know about that. It might. It might not." She looked up at the bell tower. "I used to love coming here sometimes, did you know that?"

"What happened between you and her mother?"

"Not worth talking about right now. I guess we just disagree on a few things, that's all."

A man was coming up from the center fountain of the *praça*. My mother and I studied his stride.

"She allowed her husband to kill my grandchild, that's what happened. There. Now you know. Rita was pregnant and her ignorant father made her drink this poisonous tea to get rid of the baby. And her mother was so useless. She just let him do that to her," my mother admitted, more anger in her eyes than I ever thought possible.

"Did Rita want to keep it?"

"That's hardly the point, Luca," she blurted. "But she did. She told me so herself. She cried to me many, many times. The point is Regina should've listened to her daughter, she should have stopped her husband, she should've told me, her friend and the grandmother of that baby. And she did none of that. *Católica de araque!*"

I did not see that coming at all. By the way that Rita talked, I always assumed I knew all there was to know about her. She seemed to have no secrets. Her inviting herself to my room to watch those women walk for their loved ones, their children, suddenly acquired a whole new meaning.

Across the plaza four officers strutted on horses, scanning the place. The last one in their group spun his baton like a hooker does her purse.

"Hmm," said my mother. "I'd forgotten about that. Still going…"

"But, maybe, since Pablo isn't here, maybe this was best for her. No?" I offered.

She looked at me with tired eyes.

"I don't know, *filho*. Maybe. I don't know. I know Rita had to mourn for two instead of one when it happened. I know I eventually mourned for two. I know now, if you haven't changed too much, you will also mourn for this child. How can you know if something is or is not for the best, if we always have to make the best of it?" She shrugged, and let the question sit there for a moment, like a gray storm cloud above the river, sucking up its water.

"And if I can be selfish, there isn't one day that I don't think of how different everything could have been if we had Pablo's child in our lives."

Would he or she fill the void we were left with? Would this child sprinkle our days with sudden burst of laughter, with crafty inventions, with her fears and hopes that were much bigger than all of us, a mind and a heart split between feet-on-the-ground behaviors and worldly ambitions? Would he or she be a constant reminder of what we no longer had? Did we need one?

"Well, maybe it's best she doesn't move back then?" I smiled. "You think?"

I hugged her and gave her a kiss on the cheek.

"We should get going, Mãe. I don't want you to miss your bus."

We walked back to the closest *ponto de taxi* and got into the first one. The driver listened to a re-run of that night's *Hora do Brasil* – political propaganda as strong as ever.

"Do you think Pablo knew?" I asked my mother as we waited at a red light.

She shook her head. "I know he didn't."

"Do you think it would've made any difference?" I tried.

. . .

Some days we live as if we can reinvent ourselves. As if our background can't define us. As if our past is lost somewhere far away. These days I quicken my steps as much as I can, like a criminal set free by accident, afraid that the truth will catch up to me if only I hesitate.

. . .

That evening, as she walked from Minas do Leão's bus station to their house, a crispy breeze sent chills up her core and she covered herself as much as she could with her shawl. The town was quiet. A few windows flickered with blue and pink lights from a TV set. Stray dogs curled themselves up as they sought rest and warmth.

Aside from the porch light, their house was dark and silent. Neither Mercedes nor little Junior woke up when she shut the door behind her. Neither heard the screeching sound it made when it scraped the swollen wood plank before shutting itself completely.

When my mother finally got to the back of the house, into her newly built bedroom, she sat on her bed staring out at the dark meadow, blaming herself for telling me something she shouldn't have said, for spoiling what should've been a pleasant moment. That night was not about her, and definitely not about Pablo.

She understood then why people lied about their past, why they told elaborate stories of themselves so rich in details that when repeated enough times they end up believing in them. They become their truth. That was the whole point; it was not about pleasing others, but reinvention. These people, she thought, must be happy.

Beyond her window, darkness was too deep, and the wind off the meadow, too cold for a summer night. She reached out to touch the cold red bricks on her wall. Her hands looked wrinkled and bony and old, and my mother thought she better knit herself a blanket for the coming winter.

. . .

"Sometimes I feel like he's watching me, Luca. It's weird. But I turn around and I'm just so sure that I'll see him."

Rita was sitting at the end of my bed while I was cleaning up my desk. I turned around and found her crouched, her head buried between her knees, her fingers raking through her hair.

"I'm going crazy." She flung herself back, lying on my bed. Tears streaming down to her ears.

"You're not crazy. Don't say that." I wanted to tell her how I felt the same way sometimes, to ask her if she thought Pablo could really be watching us. I wanted to know how she felt about the baby, and whether or not she had been able to forgive her parents. And Pablo.

"Today I was at this *lanchonete* eating a *pastel*, and someone was behind me, waiting, but I took a bite, and barely moved." She stopped herself to face me. "I closed my eyes," she continued, shutting her eyes. "And I was sure it was Pablo's scent that I could smell, that it was his breath that I felt on my neck. I was so sure that it was him, standing there, inches from me, and all of a sudden I felt everything." She still had her eyes closed. "As if I wasn't numb anymore. And I thought about turning around and looking at him, but the thing is, that would've been the end. And I didn't want it to end. I just didn't want it to end."

She wiped her eyes on her sleeve. "I'm pathetic, I know."

"Don't say that." I hated him for making her feel that way, for leaving her, for leaving them, us.

"I'm getting married," she announced suddenly.

"You're what?"

"I'm getting married." She sat up. We were looking at each other's eyes. "I'm engaged. We haven't set the date yet."

"I didn't, I didn't even know you were with someone." I turned my back to her, quickly realizing how upset I seemed. "Congratulations?!"

"Oh man, what am I doing?"

"You are trying to move on. Do you like him?"

"Yeah I like him." She shrugged. "But I don't know anything anymore."

I sat next to her, and wrapped my arms around her small shoulders.

"So you don't hate me?" she asked.

"*Claro que não*! Why would I?"

"Because I'm weak. Because I'm giving up. Because I sure hate myself sometimes."

I hugged her as tightly as I could.

"You are not weak. You are the most wonderful gir... most wonderful woman I know."

She forced a closed-mouth smile.

"I don't think I'm ready though."

I took her hand on mine. "Let's have a beer or six! C'mon, let's get out!"

Rita got drunk enough that night that she wanted to call it all off with her fiancé – Marcelo. Wanted to go to his house at two in the morning, tell him she didn't love him, that she wasn't ready. We shut the bar. The owner actually gave us a bottle of beer for the road, told us to come back soon. I ended up sneaking Rita back into my room and letting her sleep there.

I kept the window open to allow a night breeze inside, and enough light for me to see her. I sat on the floor and she told me how they had met, how much he had pursued her, the nice gestures that had somehow convinced her that she should give him a chance. Give herself a chance. Her words gradually slowing down, her voice becoming faint.

"You're a good friend, Luca," she whispered. She was lying on her stomach, her eyes shut. A tear spilling out of her right eye.

I just watched her, in silence, as she fell into a deep sleep. Sections of her body were illuminated by the unshadowed light post outside. One could easily argue an artist had carefully planned and placed lighting to best showcase his muse's most breathtaking features. An artist. A god. A loser. I caught myself paying attention to how her fingers would twitch every once in a while, to how the sun-kissed hairs on her arm could reflect the moonlight, to how her lips seemed fuller with her cheek pressed against the mattress, and to the loose section of her jeans on her lower back, and how when she exhaled you could see just a slit of her yellow underwear. I tried to picture her pregnant; Rita as mother, Rita as widow. I tried to remind myself of how much she needed me as a friend. But she was too beautiful. There was so much about her that was pure and innocent; a jaded angel.

The more I wished that I could keep on watching her, the more I hoped that she would call it all off with her fiancé, the sicker I felt and finally I just made myself try to get some sleep.

In the middle of the night I heard Rita mumbling something under her breath. She was lying on her side now, looking down at me from the edge of the bed.

"Were you saying something?"

"*Não, nada*. Must have been dreaming."

I fluffed up the bath towel I was using as a pillow, shut my eyes, and tried to go back to sleep. I could still sense her eyes on me.

"Marcelo doesn't like that I spend time with you." She pursed her lips, as I folded my arms under my head. "He says your presence isn't healthy for me. A reminder."

"And what do you say?"

"I don't know, Luca. I tell him he's wrong. But…" She stopped herself.

We were both quiet.

"Maybe if you two met, maybe he would change his mind."

"Doesn't sound like the guy wants to meet me," I blurted.

Rita sighed. "But you're the best thing that has happened to me ever since…, in a long time."

"Shouldn't that be your fiancé?" I sat up.

Rita shut her eyes, as if that alone could quiet her thoughts.

"Listen, Ri, you rest. Sleep it off." I draped the bath towel over the windowsill. "It's been a weird day for you…"

"What are you doing?" she asked.

"I'm just gonna go for a walk. I can't sleep anyway."

"Luca, you take the bed, I'll…"

"No, really, it's fine. I'll come back soon, you won't even notice it. Just go back to sleep."

...

Pablo, our mother had been right all along. It just took me a lot longer to realize it. But the regime did take her entire family. Every one of us lost parts of ourselves, the ones that actually made us who we were. All of us. Because of the regime I will never know what kind of man I was meant to be. And I will always fail in comparison to every man I know. Including my father.

You won't ever be the man you were meant to be, either. We have this in common, Pablo. Except you will always be better than any man I know. And this has nothing to do with what you've done with your life, and what you didn't do. It's simply because you are not here.

I trace your steps, and listen to you thoughts, the loud and quiet ones, and I try to make sense of them. I finish the thoughts you never even had a chance to conjure up, in the hopes of understanding you. And in the hopes of understanding myself.

I seek and trace any trail you might have left behind because my own tracks disappear the moment I leave them. As if my density is off, and the matter I'm made out of is too meager to leave any prints, however small.

...

Rita called me a couple days later saying she wanted to give Marcelo a 'real chance'. That she had to respect his wishes, and that she was sorry.

After hanging up with her, I left Dona Anita's place and took a bus down to Cristal, to watch the sunset. I hadn't been

160

back there in a while and I thought it would be good to clear my head.

Blue-ish-gray clouds quickly shifted across the sky as a summer storm built itself up. The whole ride I thought there wouldn't be a sunset to watch after all, and I could be lazy and not ever get out of the bus. I kept thinking of the first time Pablo ever took me there, about how much I wanted to know of him, and of life. He had sat on the bench facing the sun, like everybody else, except he didn't seem present at all, but somewhere inside his mind. The entire time I had thought what he was saying was that I had to truly understand the significance of that natural event, that I had to appreciate its magnificence as if it was part of a larger, mythical process; an initiation of sorts. And I couldn't understand why he looked *in* instead.

I got out of the bus and sat on the same bench we had sat on, under the *jacarandá* tree. The Rio Guaíba was a sluggish body of water a shade lighter than murky wet cardboard. A slit of clear sky cut through the horizon allowing the sunlight to spill over the water; a cascade of light. Scattered birds glided across the sky, taking advantage of the sudden breeze as the rainclouds shifted this way and that.

The usual types were also there, drinking their *chimarrão*, smoking their cigarettes, softly playing their acoustic guitars. On the very far right, a trio of boys passed around a joint with their cupped hands to hide the source of the smell that reached us as we all waited. Down to the left, a girl about my age stood by a *pitanga* tree, picking out and munching through its ripe fruits, as if she had come only for a snack. Her blond hair tied up in a ponytail, her skin was very pale as though she'd never been out in her life.

All of a sudden we were all hit with the sun's hot golden light straight in the eye as it sat just above the horizon. The lake immediately turned itself into a golden mirror with little silver specks of light blinking all over its surface. Everybody stopped what they were doing to study the colors around them. Everybody but the girl, who kept on picking *pitangas*, pulling down a branch rich with them, her ponytail a brighter shade of gold when hit by the sunlight.

161

So what? The sunset is beautiful? What is the point if not to numb you from all the ugliness you see everywhere else?

The sun quickly lowered itself, below the horizon, and we were left with a stripe of rich orange and pink light. Such contrast from the loaded clouds above. The amber lake gradually became rougher as the wind picked up. People started to disperse, fearing the coming rain, but I didn't feel like going home yet.

The girl, the *pitanga* eater, made her way to a rock close to me and sat down.

"You're a little late," I said.

She looked at me, somewhat surprised, then looked back at the lake.

"It's dusk that I like. I don't care for the sunset. It's too overrated. I don't like when people tell me what I should and should not find beautiful."

I smiled.

"How were the *pitangas*?"

"Pure deliciousness!" She blushed. "I want my own tree. I can't tell you how many seeds I've planted. They just don't bloom."

"Maybe it takes a while."

"Or maybe, once I have them, I won't like 'em as much."

"I doubt that."

She opened her fist revealing all the seeds she had saved. They looked like tiny wooden marbles.

"Are you planting these?"

"I don't know. Maybe I will. Maybe I'll throw them in the river."

"You know it's a lake?"

"Yeah, river, lake, whatever. Why call it Rio Guaíba then?"

"Yeah. It's silly. What's your name?"

"Mariana." She smiled.

"I'm Luca."

We walked down to the right where the trio had been and she picked a spot where the grass didn't seem as thick. We then began to dig with our bare hands. She struggled to make progress with her bitten nails and stubby fingertips. I did most of the digging myself. Fat, sparse drops of rain started to fall on

162

our backs. And I thought of my mother, and her silly belief that rain could mark the most significant changes in life, the changes we hope for.

"It's not going to grow, you know."

"Doesn't matter," I said, and kept on digging.

Without any ceremony, Mariana deposited all the seeds she had saved in her pocket. Dusk started to thicken around us. Up on the street, most cars already had their headlights on.

Mariana and I sat back on the bench. The rain was on and off, and just never really picked up, but it was enough to keep all mosquitoes away.

"So what about dusk?" I asked.

"It's not sunset." She smiled. "Besides, what's not to like?"

Yes, it was beautiful how the pink would gradually become purple, and how the purple would turn into a deeper shade of blue.

"When the sky is clear, I love to spot the very first stars. I think that's my favorite part."

We stayed for a long time. She told me she was studying to become a nurse, and that she lived in Ipanema with her father. She told me her mother was no longer around, and I couldn't tell if she had left them, or died.

"Won't your father worry about you being out late?"

She shook her head. "He goes out on Thursdays. I'm usually the one getting him back home from the *boteco*. He's not a drinker. But Thursdays are tough for him."

"Oh."

"Everyone needs a break. Thursdays are his."

"And yours?" I asked.

"I guess it would be this."

"Talking to strangers?" I smiled.

"You're Luca. Not a stranger. But I meant this. *Pitanga*, planting, dusk. I should probably find another one though. Nothing I plant ever grows." She smiled awkwardly.

...

In Santiago Pablo had food on his table, a decent job, a bed to sleep on, and Isabel, who was determined to make him forget all the horrors he had lived through by exhausting him with stories of her past, plans for their future together, and sex. Isabel was the daughter of an Italian immigrant who had made a life for himself in the capital as a carpenter. But not just any carpenter. Senhor Giuseppe specialized in wood carved furniture. Rocking chairs, leaf-tables with detailed pedestal legs, candle stands… Art pieces; everything he created would go through different generations of families, different eras. He had hired Pablo to help him with the basics, but when he saw what he was capable of doing, Senhor Giuseppe started to treat him as his apprentice, and soon invited him home for dinner. Isabel hadn't left Pablo's side since. Every time Senhor Giuseppe blinked, she'd be hanging onto my brother's neck.

"Papa says he wants to teach you how to carve. He's never taught anybody before, you know? Not even my brother." Isabel traced his lips with her fingertip, then smoothed each of his eyebrows. Pablo almost fell asleep on her lap, a black and white TV hummed on the background.

"But that one will lose at least four fingers before he gets through his first table. *Ai ai ai.*" She laughed.

Sometimes, when Isabel laughed, she'd look up and hold her stomach as if trying to contain herself; reminding him of Rita, of how easily Rita could cry with laughter. And of how much he loved to make her laugh. Sometimes, he loved that about Isabel. Sometimes, he hated it.

. . .

"I'm tired, Pa," I say. "I can't do this anymore."

The smell of sulfur is so soothing.

"Neither can I." A whisper in the mine's damp darkness.

"I have looked everywhere. I've tried everything. I can't find you. Why don't you just tell me where you are? Why don't you just tell me what happened?"

"It wasn't me you were looking for. We both know this," says Pablo.

"But it was also you."

A beam of light frantically moves up, down, right, left; all directions.

An old man in a hard hat walking with a cane appears in the darkness. His shaky hand can barely hold the flashlight.

"The mine has been shut, Senhor. It's been shut for decades now," he says. "You can't be here. You need to leave immediately."

"My father used to work here."

"I know," he says. "I knew your family."

THIRTEEN

IT WAS A sticky January afternoon, and I was enjoying my final days off by spending as much time with Vitória as I could. Pretty soon I'd return to teach every morning while she attended school in the afternoons. Pelé napped lazily underneath our *pitangueira*, occasionally wagging his tail to brush off a fly, or to simply swipe it through Vi's leg. Vitória pulled down on the one branch she could reach, using her six-year-old fingers to test the ripeness of each fruit. That was the summer that she had discovered her passion for *pitangas*, a passion that seemed greater than her mother's. But she was only then getting acquainted with the fruit, and had no shame in crying for them, in getting upset with a tree for being such a slow, incompetent producer, oblivious to her own needs, and in jumping for joy when I imported a bunch from another tree around the neighborhood. I loved watching her. There was much grace in the way she carried herself, and yet if you looked closely you could still spot the little idiosyncrasies that took me right back to the day I had met her mother.

"Got one!" she yelled and did a happy dance, stepping on Pelé's paw, who simply withdrew his limb and went back to sleep.

I walked up to the still quite short tree, and pulled down some of the branches she couldn't reach. Vitória folded her tank top at her stomach, using it as a pocket for everything I handed to her.

"Can we eat them all?" she asked with her big hazel eyes when I was done.

"*Sim*, let's just wash them first."

I turned on the faucet, grabbed the hose and brought it close to her. She watched me attentively, trying to guess what the plan was.

"We can wash them one by one, or all at once. What do you say?" I asked.

"All!"

I cocked my head to the side and looked at her, waiting for a confirmation. She nodded and I soaked her pocketed tank top; the *pitangas* circling around, floating in the little pool she had made for them, and Vitória laughed hysterically. Pelé got up and found another shaded spot to sleep, away from the water. His large paws left prints on the puddled dirt.

As we sat on the porch to eat, I could hear the hum of Mariana's soap opera from the living room. She liked her siesta after lunch, and she liked the constant hum as well as the exaggerated inflections the actors would bring to our house. For her, a silent home lacked life.

Outside, sudden gusts of wind shook the leaves of our new avocado tree and made the sheets on the triple line dance and tangle then untangle themselves again as if performing for us. The hairs on Vitória's forearm stuck up and she scooted over to my side. She chose two maroon-colored *pitangas*, carefully picking them out so she wouldn't bruise their skin. One for each of us. When I was done I spit out the seed, while I watched Pelé roll over, his entire white fur covered in dust, his stomach facing the sky, pink with little brown spots, and his legs spread out, trusting.

"How do you do that?" she asked.

"Do what?"

"Spit like that."

"You really want to know?" I asked.

Vitória nodded without hesitation.

"Alright. You make your tongue into a 'U' shape. Like this," I said and stuck my tongue out.

She did the same with hers.

"Yes, like that." I said. "Keep the seed not on the tip of your tongue, but a little farther in. Careful not to swallow, okay? Or else a pitanga tree will grow in your belly. Then you take a deep breath, through your nose." She nodded, attentively. "And when you spit, bring all that air out. Like an explosion!"

She smiled and gave it a try. Laughing awkwardly when she

realized how much saliva had come out with the seed.

"You can use your body to help too. Think of your body and tongue as a catapult."

She looked at me, and I showed her what I had meant.

"Okay," she said.

Her second attempt was a lot better than the first.

"What are you two doing?" Mariana asked, leaning against the frame of our front door. Her eyes squinting as they tried to adapt to so much light.

"Papai is teaching me how to spit very far!" our daughter announced as she got up to look at Mariana.

"Lovely, I've been meaning to teach you myself," she said, looking at me in disbelief.

"We're planting!" I offered.

"Oh well, you two behave yourselves. I gotta wash the dishes." Mariana walked back into the house, turning up the volume of the TV enough to hear it from the kitchen.

Vitória kept on practicing as she got through the bunch we had picked. With every seed, it seemed she went over, in her head, each of the steps I had described to her before attempting to reenact them.

Pelé, realizing her aim wasn't all that great, decided to drag himself to my side. My foot, a pillow for his fuzzy head. Just the tip of his tongue sticking out from his under bite.

"Can we pick more after?"

The phone rang inside, and I heard Mariana's clogs rushing across our living room.

"It'll give you a tummy ache," I said. "Tomorrow we'll do this again."

"Can I wash those and do it again?" She pointed at a few of the seeds scattered through our front yard.

I shook my head. "We've planted them. We can't…"

"Luca, who is Rita?" Mariana asked from the front door.

"What?" I hadn't seen Rita since her wedding.

"Who is Rita? Someone named Rita on the phone for you?"

she said. "She seems a little rude."

"Not sure. The only one I know used to be Pablo's girlfriend I told you about. But I doubt she has our number, though."

"Uncle Pablo, *papai?*"

"*Sim,* love. Uncle Pablo," I answered, and went in.

"Hello?" The receiver wet from Mariana's hand.

"Luca!"

"Rita? Hi! How are you? Are you okay?"

"Yes. My mother asked your mother for your phone number. I hope it's okay to call your house. Your wife sounds lovely, by the way. That was your wife, right?"

Mariana sat down with our daughter. Pelé sat himself up, stretching his neck, hoping she would pet him on the chest.

"Are you watching it?" I could hear her shallow breathing over the receiver.

"Watching what?"

"Turn the TV on, right now!" she said. "You're not gonna believe it!"

Several times, I had thought of rekindling our friendship, of introducing our spouses and children, if she had had any. I had hoped that she would one day talk to Vitória about her uncle, about the sides of Pablo that only Rita got to see.

"Alright, would you like to wait on the line?"

"No, no! I'll catch you later!"

"Sounds good."

"*Beijo.*"

I hung up and walked across the living room, Rita's words ringing in my ears. Different scenarios flashed through my mind in that short amount of time. Whatever it was, it had to be big for her to call me. And I suddenly felt the heat around my temples as if for the first time in that steamy afternoon, almost instantaneously becoming unbearable. I pictured a spokesperson listing out the names of those who had disappeared, taking responsibility, or a local reporter announcing they had found a body, or maybe the list of rebels who were granted amnesty and could finally return home from exile. All the things we would constantly hear someone demanding to happen, hoping, praying that another someone would listen.

Pushing on the channel buttons, it didn't take long to land on what she must have meant, and I took a seat. On the screen I found a huge sea of people marching, sweating under the same unforgiving sun as ours. The reporter announced there were about three hundred thousand of them, taking over Praça da Sé, in São Paulo. I hadn't seen anything as big in my entire life. They walked slowly with nervous smiles, but smiles nonetheless. Their pockets, filled with marbles, weighted down by a burden they haven't asked for. A mass of pride, patriotism, commitment, and scars conquered the avenues with locked arms, as they chanted their mantra over and over.

The reporter would rush through his sentences, aware they could be cut at any minute, aware that what they were broadcasting was forbidden and on a ticking clock. They would cut from live action and show photos and a couple of videos of previous protests which had already taken place earlier in the month across the country. Images that hadn't been made public until then. And between this going back and forth from São Paulo to Salvador, to Goiás, to Belo Horizonte, and all these other cities, I noticed how as they walked, people took turns in holding banners as wide as the avenues they were about to overcome. Its massive size carried the weight of its message, of the past, and of their role in creating our future. It was then that I finally saw Pablo again. On January 25th, 1984, I saw my brother's words at all corners of our country, and I finally realized how much hope they bore in them, as people lined up to carry the banners at the protests' forefront. In their faces, in the way some of them hunched over, or how their adam's apple would bulge as they chanted, or the way some of them would crack up at some side joke we couldn't hear... in each of those people I found the pieces I had searched for, and struggled for most of my life to understand.

Vitória's skinny arm hooked around mine as she laid her head on my shoulder. Her hair still wet from playing with the hose. When I turned to face her, I realized Mariana was standing right behind me, watching the both of us.

"What is it, *papai*?" she whispered softly. "Why are you crying?"

How could I ever explain what that meant, and what I was feeling watching his message become an anthem for our youth, this new generation of hopeful, fearless protesters?

This would be the first of many televised marches countrywide as part of the Diretas Já movement. Information regarding a proposed amendment had leaked, fueling everyone's hopes, as Congress prepared itself to vote on reestablishing direct Presidential elections. And seeing how our Congress just as quickly tried to pull all sorts of tricks to postpone this vote, hopeful men and women, boys and girls, realized their responsibility in this final battle. That same square in São Paulo would receive 1.5 million protesters in April. People would protest from their windows, sidewalks, or just follow the mass. They'd chant, they'd dance, some would cry, others would laugh, but Pablo's message, "THEY CAN'T SHUT US UP!" would always be in bold, capital letters, projecting the crowds forward. Their voices would echo against the taller buildings; a wave of resilience, of innocence and faith.

I was surprised they kept on broadcasting the whole thing. I kept waiting for a black or a silver screen to pop up. But on that day, nothing was done. No retaliation. No response whatsoever. If you looked closely at each of the protesters' faces, you could clearly see fear in their eyes, but somehow hope was what they projected.

Vitória caressed my face with such tenderness, I felt I was corrupting her by showing pain, by crying in front of my daughter who I wished would only experience beauty, and peace and happiness in her life.

"*Amor*, iced water?" asked Mariana with a tall glass in her hand.

We looked at each other for a moment. My eyes begged that she would tell me what I should say to our daughter, hoping she would help me say only the right things and nothing that could scare or scar her. Her eyes and soft smile seemed tranquil and confident.

"You know, you should tell her." She nodded. "Some day you should tell her."

ACKNOWLEDGMENTS

A short story version of *The Marble Army* appeared in *Expressionists*. Thank you to John Struloeff and the editors for believing in this project long before I did.

I am indebted to my professors and classmates at Queens University of Charlotte for their insight, guidance and inspiration. To Pinckney Benedict and Naeem Murr whose comments were especially helpful in the shaping of this book. To Fred Leebron, my agent, tireless professor and friend extraordinaire, for his generosity, honesty and for continuously pushing me beyond my own limitations. To Jon Roemer, editor and publisher of this volume, for his belief, kindness and wisdom.

Above all, I am deeply grateful to my husband, Luciano, who has read and listened to almost every version. Thanks to my parents for their love and support, Vó Anita for inspiration, the folks in Minas do Leão and the many witnesses who were so generous to share their experiences with me. Finally, to my son Lorenzo, who reminds me everyday to never underestimate the power of the good guys.

photo credit: Meinel Waldow

Gisele Firmino earned a BA from Pepperdine University and an MFA in Fiction from Queens University of Charlotte. Born and raised in the south of Brazil, Gisele's writing has appeared in such journals as *Expressionists* and *Rose & Thorn*. She works as a freelance translator and lyricist and is also the founding locale coordinator for Queens University's MFA in Creative Writing: Latin America. She currently divides her time between Brazil and the United States. *The Marble Army* is her first novel.

CPSIA information can be obtained at www.ICGtesting.com
Printed in the USA
BVOW02s0858040216

435493BV00001B/1/P